Parallel WORLDS

BOOK ONE

Also by Clark Kneuker

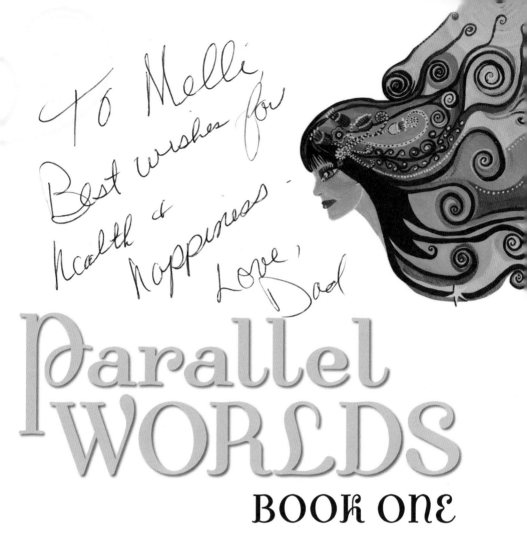

To Melli,
Best wishes for
health &
happiness
Love,
Dad

Parallel
WORLDS

BOOK ONE

CLARK KNEUKER

Cover and Interior artwork by Patricia Jepsen

Cover and Interior design by Candice M. Carta-Myers

Dedication

DR. JOHN MANHOLD

I am so very fortunate to know John, one of the more brilliant men on our planet. I admire his boundless energy and pursuit of excellence in everything he does. Although John is wonderfully accomplished in writing, sculpture, music, marksmanship, and medicine, his original desire was teaching English. Even with a heavy workload, he coached me through plays, bad poetry, and the outset of this novel. I will always greatly appreciate his encouragement, straightforward criticisms, and breadth of knowledge. His support is enduring and his pursuit of excellence is incomparable.

Contents

Foreword

Prepare to travel to other dimensions where Historical facts meet Science fiction . . . Religious facts meet fantasy.

Open your mind and examine your Soul. Be on your guard, and know that an enemy is determined to exploit you.

He or she may appear as better than your best friend ever has.

So, strap yourself in and imagine a gateway opening up right before your eyes.

—CLARK KNEUKER, AUTHOR

"Come Fairies, take me out of this dull world, for I would ride with you upon the wind and dance upon the mountains like a flame!"

—WILLIAM BUTLER YEATS

"We must ask whether the abnormal phenomena which have been so frequently discussed, fought over, forgotten, and revived, **do not** enter into the general mass of folk lore. Thus all Fairydom was commonly looked on as under the guilt of witchcraft. Yet Mr. Kirk of Aberfoyle, living among Celtic people, treats the land of the fairy as a mere fact in nature, a world with its own laws, which he investigates without fear of the Accuser of the Brethren."

—ANDREW LANG

"This is a rebellious people, which say to the seers, see not; and to the prophets, prophesy not unto us right things, but speak to us smooth things."

—ISAIAH 30:10

Preface

Several decades ago, I was sitting with my partner, Sgt. Fred Avalos, in a radio jeep near Khe Sahn, Vietnam. It was the middle of the night; we were a few miles from the DMZ when we witnessed a plane very high in the sky. We saw one plane and then we saw two; within moments, we saw perhaps a dozen and then fifty or more. Were we witnessing an invasion? We were spooked for a moment until we realized the planes were stars and a cloud was passing by. After that moment, I realized that I would prefer writing as a career.

Many years passed until I retired to pursue that dream. I was very fortunate to know one of the more brilliant men on the planet. Dr. John Manhold married my wife's lovely Aunt Kitty. Despite John's wonderful accomplishments in writing, sculpture, music, and medicine, his great passion was that of an English teacher. He coached me with plays and bad poems until he suggested that I write a book. He liked a passage I wrote about a fairy queen. Kit liked my writing too.

I thought about writing fantasy, but truth is stranger than fiction. One restless night, either I had an out-of-body experience, or was abducted by extraterrestrials. Either way, I travelled through space and time; unlike most people, I ended up on a branch in a massive pine tree in Scotland. There I met Minister Robert E. Kirk, his soul still incarcerated since 1692, his spirit still upbeat.

Although he had been there over three centuries, he had not yet given up his dream. Of course, I listened to his story after he complained vociferously about how stupid people had become in the modern world. He went on and on about how many souls were going to hell and how frustrated he was. He had done so much work in studying *fairies*, the *sleigh maithe* and *siths* as he preferred to call them, with a hiss in his voice as if they were snakes.

I told him that I would like to write a book about him and tell his side of the story. He prayed for me; it was nothing like I ever heard before. I learned that it took over a hundred years for his book to reach the market; that simply writing it cost him his life and got him locked up in that damn tree. He frightened me a bit. I asked the man upstairs to look out for me.

Years later, I completed four novels to get the whole story out there. *Parallel Worlds* will take you with the minister as he discovers the unthinkable. In *Connected Worlds* and *Worlds Reconnected*, you will travel with an ancestor on a rescue mission followed by an endless pursuit of a relentless archenemy, those *fairies, sleigh maithe* or *siths*.

I must say, the foretelling of the future in *Final Connection* came to me very strangely; I dare not give the source. I must assume full responsibility for the release of this story. Your prayers are greatly appreciated. I visited the tree; while there's a wonderful view from there, it's not where I would like to spend eternity. All I can say is that the conflict will be resolved and what happens in this book will come true. I pray this information serves you well.

Clark Kneuker

Parallel WORLDS

BOOK ONE

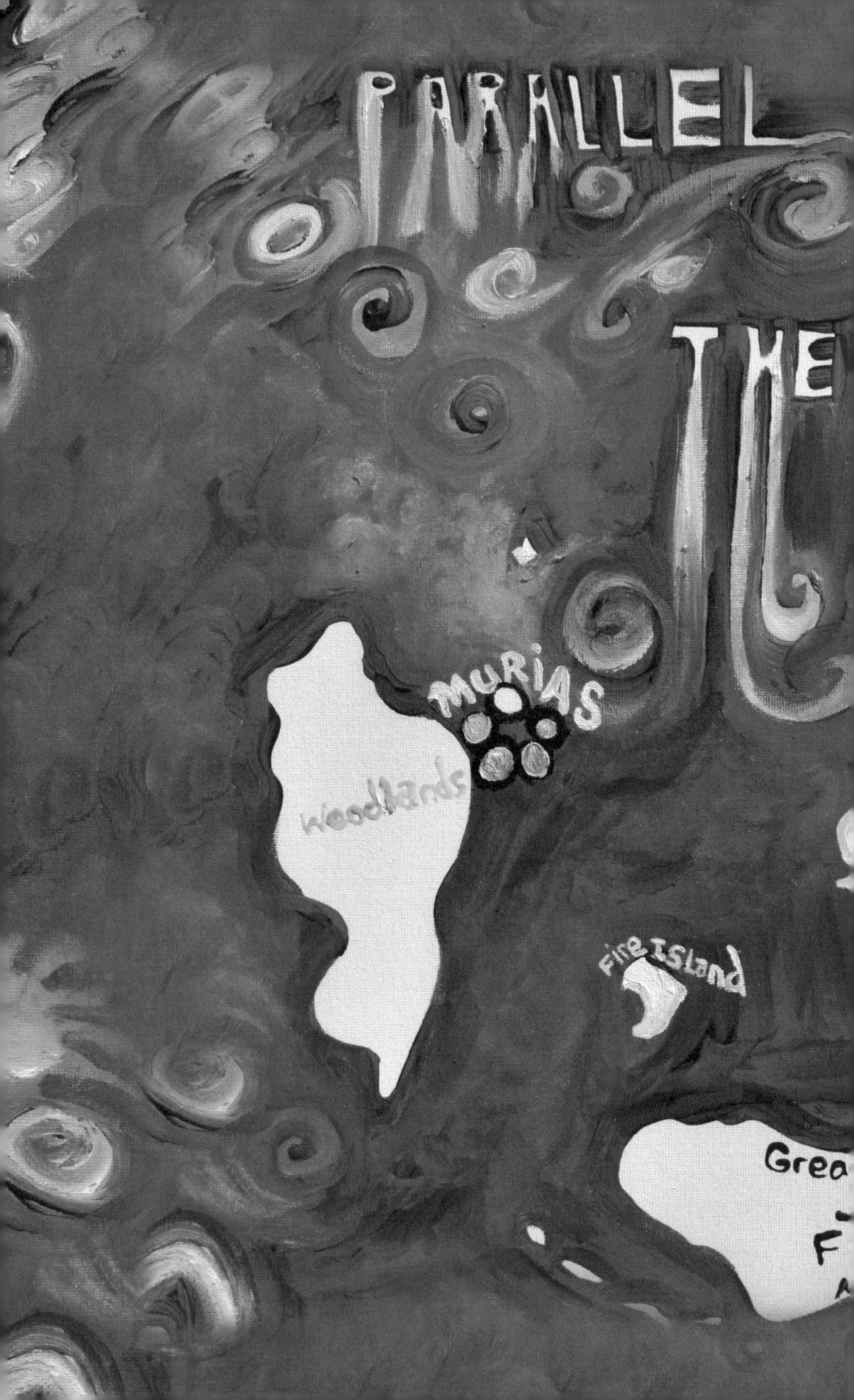
PARALLEL
THE
MURIAS
Woodlands
Fire Island
Grea

Aberfoyle
Scotland
1692

CHAPTER 1

The Incarceration

"I see disbelievers amongst you," boldly stated Minister Kirk from his pulpit, his close-knit eyes causing a few men and their wives to squirm on the hard wooden pews, "not disbelievers of God, but disbelievers in me. Some of you are afraid of my mission to stop the *siths*; others of you do not believe my reports. The *sleigh maithe* nay the fair folk have existed on this earth longer than we have. Their bodies of congealed air are sometimes carried aloft; otherwhiles grovel in different shapes, and enter into any cranny or cleft of the earth to their ordinary dwellings, the earth being full of cavities and cells. No creature is supposed to live upon another as an inhabitant, but there's no such thing as a pure wilderness in the whole universe."

The minister paused to look up and stare at his congregation; he then continued, "Fairies have no discernible religion or devotion to God and have nothing of the Bible. They have held anger with God ever since Lilith, Adam's first wife from medieval Jewish text. Who was this woman Lilith? She no longer appears in Genesis; scholars either were not able to grasp her reality or explain the contradiction of Eve as the first woman. Lilith was a beautiful specimen, voluptuous, sensual, and shrewd, more than capable to be the mother of man. She had everything except one thing; she had no soul. She was lacking in the only difference between them and us; the soul is the reason for our existence and creation." Again, he paused and looked around the church as if he were looking for some disagreement or even something else.

"When God rejected Lilith as the mother of man she became outraged. She swore to her people that she would do everything to avenge her annulment; she made a promise to take the soul from man, and give this gift of eternal life to the good

3

people, the superior race. In her rage, she caused abortions and inflicted diseases on babies. Ultimately, she settled for baby abductions to obtain healthy slaves for her world. Combined with the abductions, she began the despicable practice of leaving behind changelings, the rejected, often deformed, and imperfect babies of their species. Sadly, changelings exist with neither fair folk nor human folk caring for them."

"All fair folk were angry with God for not choosing Lilith," he continued. "They were certain that God had created a soul for them. As a result, Lilith led the charge for fairies to steal the soul and make it their own. Lilith convinced them all that it was necessary for their survival."

"Fear not brethren; strengthen your soul and you will achieve God's purpose in his expansive universe. Heaven is your destiny."

The minister paused again. No one could look at him; they all felt urgency in his voice and knew this sermon was something they needed to hear. While there was very little skepticism, there was much fear in the minds of the congregation. This invisible enemy had powers beyond their imagination. When an enemy is capable of stealing an infant from a mother's breast, they could do anything.

Not one person sitting in the pews doubted Minister Kirk, for he was a seventh son and had the gift of second sight; he could see the sneaky astral spirits preying on the population. Not only was he able to see what fairies were doing, he wrote down everything in a matter-of-fact manner. He gave explanation to the terror in their lives, described them, and documented their behavior just as an educated farmer would record his spring planting and the progress of his plants. Most impressive, was Minister Kirk's ability to see doppelgangers, body doubles that were the spitting image of their human counterparts. They always fled from the body before death. Because of this, Minister Kirk was able to predict when a member of his community was about to die.

Not only that, Kirk was fearless with this enemy. Even though his wife was pregnant with their fourth child and could be a target of their anger, he spoke against them. The congregation knew he was a truthful well-intentioned man and was correct in everything he said. He quoted the Bible to support his claims. No one had studied the Bible more than him for he was the first person to translate the Bible into Gaelic.

He was their greatest hope and their worst fear. Their hope was that he could protect them and stop the enemy. They were terrified that he would make fairies angry and they would take their anger out on the congregation. While Kirk could refer to them as *sleigh maithe* or *siths,* the townspeople respectfully and fearfully referred to them as good folk or fair folk. It was not wise to upset them.

Minister Kirk continued, "God's gift to man is the soul and the opportunity for eternal life. The *siths* will attach themselves to your body and do everything within their power to steal your soul. The deer scents out a man and powder from a great distance. As a man of second sight and your humble minister, I perceive the operations of these invisible people amongst us; I observe them in their fairy hills. They steal babies from their mother's breast when she dozes off for a second."

Pausing to allow his congregation to calm down, he continued, "They attach themselves to the sick and dying to track their souls passing from this life. A co-walker or reflex man is what they call this spirit. In every way, this spirit is like a twin brother haunting the original before he is dead. I can see them at their evil intervention. Protect yourself with an iron weapon for they are terrified by nothing on earth, so much as cold iron."

Minister Kirk stopped abruptly. He was shocked - one of them, a double-man in his own image, was standing proudly just inside the front door in total defiance. The minister was quick and decisive. He drew an iron knife from his belt and heaved it at the ghostly intruder, invisible to the others.

"In the name of God the Father and his only son Jesus, I command you to leave this holy site," demanded the minister.

The double-man stood horrified as the knife passed through his astral body and struck the church door. With horror in his eyes, the fairy realized he had avoided certain death. The ghostly spirit smiled briefly as he bowed his head and floated out a window.

"Fear not, those parishioners new to my church and those that know and trust me well. A co-walker, this vile double-man just appeared before me to harass and mock my message to you. His mortal fear of iron has chased him from our presence. I am not intimidated by them and their harassment."

He paused a moment and glared at them, "It is your duty to strengthen your soul. God has a greater plan for you. A strong soul requires a strong will, and it is our only protection against unseen forces. Tonight I ask for your prayers as I embark on a mission to hold fairies accountable for the sadness and misery they have inflicted on our people. '*They disappear whenever they hear reference to God or the name of Jesus (at which all do bow willingly or by constraint that dwell above or beneath within the earth,* (Philippians 2:10).' Let us pray."

Such was the sermon for Minister Robert E. Kirk on the spring morning of 14 May 1692. After a passionate plea leaving every parishioner of the congregation exhausted, Kirk spoke to each member as they left his small church in Aberfoyle, Scotland.

He then returned to the altar to pray and review his plan for the evening. His heart pulsed with excitement for he felt strong and confident about succeeding in his mission. He would find an opening to walk into their world. The moon would be full; ground fog would provide him cover; entering the parallel world was within his grasp. Foremost in his mind, the fairies, after a day of nefarious behavior, would no longer be able to hide from him.

When Minister Kirk returned to his home, he found his wife in the garden selecting lilacs for the table. They walked together to their home. The aroma of lamb stew greeted him at the door. On this spring evening, his sanctuary felt even more special. During grace at the dinner table, he was especially thankful for his healthy wife, Margaret, soon to give birth to their fourth child. The minister was emotional as he also prayed for his three boys: Colin, age twelve, and William, age eleven from a previous marriage, and his youngest son Robert E. Kirk Jr, age two. After dinner, the minister tucked the younger Robert in bed and spent some time with his boys.

"Will you tell us about the fairy folk?" asked Colin.

"Tell us about them," added William, "tell us a tale about your adventures with them. What do they look like?"

"They are somewhat of the nature of a condensed cloud and can be seen more clearly in the twilight," replied the minister. "That's why I study them in the evening on Doon Hill, known as Fairy Knowe in their world. Listen to me, boys. Whilst the good folk seem gentle enough, never let them in for they are robbers and will steal your soul; you must be vigilant. The unborn child your mother carries is in danger of their despicable behavior. Let us not speak of them any more today. Please close your eyes and say your prayers. Make certain you pray for the safety of your unborn sibling and your mother's health. Give God thanks for this wonderful day."

The minister gave each one a kiss on the forehead, said a prayer, and stood watching them for a few moments. His thoughts were on making his world a safer place for his children and the very serious task ahead of him. He left the boys and donned his nightgown as well as his boots; it was his usual practice before making his way to Doon Hill. He kissed Margaret on the cheek and felt their baby kick inside her belly.

"Why don't you stay at home with me this evening?" pleaded his wife. "It's foggy and damp. You have seen enough of fairy folk for one day. Leave them alone or they will cause us problems. The baby's birth and christening will be soon; I don't want them interfering with God's work."

"I'm doing God's work," countered the minister. "I've never done anything else. My Bible translation clarifies many misinterpretations. I must inform everyone about this enemy who is determined to steal our soul. I had a troublesome visitor today at service."

"Tell me what happened."

"A double-man appeared; he was my duplicate. I gave him a taste of iron he will not soon forget. Bold and defiant he stood until my blade pierced his astral spirit."

"Did you frighten away your congregation?"

"They know I protect them and they know the good folk or fair folk are afraid of me. My book will go a long way to stopping the abductions of our babies."

"There's nothing good or fair about them," said his wife. "I know I can't stop you, but I worry so. Please be careful; always have your knife handy, and use it like you did today."

"They know I'll use my knife," said the minister. "It's a strange parallel world in which we live. God is sending me on a mission to protect our world. He will open the door for me. Do not fear for me, good wife. In the evening amongst the mist, fairies think of me as a spirit; what is alive that is also dead makes them afraid of me. They have no grasp of the soul. Ghosts terrify them."

"I'm afraid for our children," said Margaret. "Robert Jr. will certainly follow your ways. I would go mad if my baby was stolen from me."

"Be calm, wife, I know you don't support me. I'm doing this to stop their criminal behavior."

"I understand. Please be careful. Think about your unborn child."

Kirk walked out of his house in his nightgown. Through the fog, he could see the moon was full and everything was as he expected. Light radiated around the shadows of pine trees. He walked directly to his church located in a line of sight across a field to Doon Hill/Fairy Knowe.

Opening the chapel door, he paused to enter, as was his usual routine. The serenity of the moonlight filtering through the windows lifted his spirit; his soul felt strong with a sense of calmness. Entering the church, he kneeled at the altar and thanked God for the confidence given to him. After a few minutes, he sighed deeply for stress had left his body. He smiled a reverent smile that remained on his face until the moment he left the church. When the door closed behind him, he assumed the focus of a hunter.

A serious look came over his face; his heart raced with anticipation. Gazing across the field through the ground fog, he imagined what he would see when finally looking into Fairy Knowe.

Raising his arms, he assumed the posture of a ghost and began crossing the field. In his mind, he followed a ritual of clearing the space of the field and the hill of any evil presence. Through the ground fog, he could see fairies making their way to return home before nightfall. Thinking of himself as a ghost, he moved his arms from side to side, groaning loudly in such a way as to challenge every fairy in the field and on the hill.

As he moved across the field like an apparition, ground fog slowly became more of a mist in the twilight. With the moon rising, he could see the hill was mostly covered by a cloud, except for one tree at the very top, his destination. The massive pine tree at the center of the hill, known as the Fairy Tree, towered above every other tree. This evening it looked as if it was small and floating on the cloud.

It was at the base of this tree where he had discovered fairies rushing to return to their world at the end of each day. On this night, his mission was to hurry them along, chase them into their world disguised as a ghost and follow them right into Fairy Knowe. The conditions were perfect; he was executing his plan to perfection. At the base of the hill, he started up the main path and intensified his pursuit.

Unknowingly, Minister Kirk was rushing into a trap. Khalen, the tenth Fairy King of the region and the great city of Falias since the reign of Lilith, had built a palace into the hill of Fairy Knowe. He had been studying Minister Kirk and had sent the double-man earlier that day.

Khalen was under great duress from leaders of the three other major cities and regions in his world. King Odin of Gorias, Lady Vivienne from Murias, and Brighid, the Sun Goddess, from Finias, all pressured Khalen to stop Minister Kirk from writing his book. It was one thing for humans to talk and preach about them, but this minister was accurately writing everything down and creating a blueprint for others to follow. He was getting closer and closer to them every day making him a more and more dangerous threat. Their worse fear was materializing before their eyes and King Khalen was seemingly allowing an invasion to ensue. An army of human folk carrying iron weapons would be just as indefensible as the invasion of North America by the Europeans.

Unlike the other leaders, Khalen had a viable plan to steal the human soul. He was more interested in capturing Minister Kirk than stopping him. Khalen developed a plan to draw in Minister Kirk and trap him with ropes. He would study the minister with the hope of taking his soul. Khalen's main concern was making certain to avoid the iron weapon. He was not afraid of a one-man invasion.

In the Fairy Knowe garden, at the base of the massive pine tree, Khalen made an announcement to his guards as Kirk was traversing across the field.

"The minister will be amongst us very soon," stated the king, his steely gray eyes focused and intense. "He is disguised as a ghost. The fool is in his nightgown. Unlike other ghosts, you will recognize his offensive green aura. The aura emanates from an iron weapon in his possession. Although you will fear him, you must lead him to me. When he reaches the base of the hill, I will issue a red alert."

"From the meteoric rock," he continued, "a burst of electromagnetic energy in the form of a red light wave will pulse along the earth's grid. It will have two effects. You will feel a boost of energy; Minister Kirk will experience something completely different. I have targeted the energy to a focal point in his mind; it will exacerbate his fears. While he is a threat to our world, and a potential invader, his death is unacceptable. We will not harm him, but capture him with these ropes. I do not want a martyr; I do want his soul. My love for you is powerful. Trust in me and we will prevail. Love conquers all things and death before dishonor is our code. We will capture Minister Kirk when he enters our world."

Armed with the power of earth's electromagnetic energy, King Khalen had been targeting the human mind for centuries. His technology was constantly improving. Fairies believed he was telekinetic. He assisted Odin, Vivienne, and Brighid in controlling their human population – those babies abducted to become laborers. His technology targeted the human mind, keeping humans happy as laborers and a subservient race. As long as the leaders met every human need, human folk served their masters with smiles on their faces. While God created humans to serve him, Khalen had successfully brainwashed this inferior species to serve fair folk. The king was convinced he could influence Kirk's mind to succumb to fear and become disoriented. He would capture the minister regardless of an iron knife.

Khalen wanted to be the first to acquire a human soul. The hope on this day was to capture Minister Kirk, take him as a prisoner, and eventually possess his soul. The minister's record keeping would stop; there would be no book, and the townspeople would never talk about him again for fear of fairy retaliation.

As soon as Kirk started up the path, he made eye contact with several fairies attempting to hide in the mist through the trees. He glared at them and accelerated his ghostly assault. Running wildly up the winding narrow path, he made groaning sounds. Sound coming from a dead person always confused and terrified them. The red wave began pulsing from the earth's grid along the path.

At the first small tree where the path twisted to his left, he felt a sting in his chest. The image of his first wife Isobel crossed his path. He quickly identified the fake as her body double; she mocked him by puckering her lips. Kirk groaned louder at the astral being; the apparition moved quickly up the hill, frightened that the minister had figured out her game, yet excited by the red pulsing energy.

Kirk began thinking about the death of his first wife and the threat of losing Margaret and their unborn child. Another pang in his chest struck him causing him to stumble, nearly falling twice making a turn around a tree on the path. He became more determined than ever to stop this enemy.

As he neared the top of the hill, thoughts about his life swept through his mind like images from a book. He felt yet another pang, this one a small quake. He thought about the first day when he had discovered his gift of second sight. That fairy was astonished and became so afraid. He felt so powerful at the time. This energized him; he continued up the hill keeping his arms outstretched, making his best impression of a ghost. His heart raced; his face turned red and he became more and more excited with the chase.

Rounding a final tree to the top, he saw the image of his second wife, Margaret, not carrying his fourth child, but rather holding his third son, Robert E. Kirk Jr. and looking angry.

"You will bring disgrace upon our family with this fairy nonsense," she said. "Good hearted women have been called witches and burned alive for less than what you're doing. These fairy folk are demons and they could harm our child to make us all pay."

This body-double faded away and another appeared. He was an old friend and parishioner who died while Kirk was trying to help him repel an evil spirit. That ordeal had been exhausting and reminded Kirk of his friend's untimely death. Remorse and grief once again touched the minister's heart. He gave a ghostly scream at the apparition; again, the spirit fled from him.

Nearly breathless, he started the steepest push to the massive pine tree thinking that the window to the parallel world would be open to him. The strange red glow coming from under the earth along the path intensified. This was unexpected. Fear of failing entered his mind. A sharp twinge struck him in his chest. His life flashed before his eyes even more quickly. He remembered the day he learned about being the seventh son of his father; he remembered Reverend Robert Blair at St. Andrews healing a patient with scrofula (tuberculosis) with the power of touch. Thoughts about the Bible gave him more courage so he continued his charade. Fairy folk were ahead of him rushing into the portal. Some looked back at him with fear in their eyes; others taunted him.

With a few more strides, he saw exactly what he was hoping for; the gateway was open. Standing in lush grass with rose bushes in the background was King Khalen in red military clothing. He had pure white hair, steely gray eyes wide-opened, and a broad smile. Kirk felt another sharper pain, a larger quake in his chest. He charged ahead maintaining his ghostly charade, forgetting all about his knife. Another massive stroke hit him; death had a grip on his heart. Realizing that something was very wrong, his mind played a scene as time slowed down:

As a ghost, he went to the home of his dear, most trusted cousin. "Graham!" he called out. "Hear me well! The sleigh maithe have captured me. A thrown knife is my only hope of breaking their hold on me. Throw the knife when the time comes! It will be my one chance to escape them!"

"I give my word to do this for you," replied Graham opening his eyes in horror.

All of this happened in an instant; Kirk clutched at his heart and collapsed in the portal before Khalen.

The body of Reverend Kirk along with his knife dropped out of the portal; he lay lifeless at the base of the pine tree on Doon Hill. Trapped in the portal in a vortex of electromagnetic energy, the minister got glimpses of his body on one side of the portal and glimpses of Khalen on the other side. He was cognizant of his soul.

"Minister Kirk, you are charged with invasion and terrorism," stated King Khalen. "Your book has made you a threat to our existence. You are undeserving of a soul. Your ministry is a threat to our world. We have tolerated you long enough. While death was not my plan, you will serve us well."

"Jesus will defend my soul," shouted the minister, now accepting his death.

"Perhaps," countered Khalen, "but you are in my custody and in my domain. I am King Khalen and I rule the region of Falias, the oldest city of earth built of granite and precious stones. My city represents earth and its power. I now have your soul locked in with the electromagnetic energy of the earth. There is no escape; look back upon your body. You look foolish lying there in your nightgown and wearing boots."

"God will punish you," said the minister. "You are evil to steal babies from their mother's breast."

"We are a more worthy species than you," said Khalen. "We take better care of your children than you do. Once your soul becomes mine, God will see that my species is more worthy of eternal life and heaven. You humans are so confused and reckless with life. Evil lurks in many of your souls. Some of you do not even believe in the soul. We believe that love conquers all things; you believe in your weapons."

"You even discard your own babies. Our weapons defend us against your brand of evil. You will never have a soul," countered Kirk. "It's not the will of God."

"Are you not listening to me? I have **your** soul," retorted Khalen. "It is just a matter of time before I make it my own."

"The soul is not of the physical," said Kirk.

"That is where you are wrong," said Khalen. "While its mass and electrical charge is small, your gene resided deep within your DNA. It escaped your body when you died and I now control you. You could never understand its nature."

"I understand its power; that is something you could never understand."

"Let us see your power, then," said the fairy king. "Break away from me."

Reverend Kirk slumped forward.

Continuing through the gateway, the reverend could not fight the hold that gripped him. He was in a spinning web that continued to tighten. Although he was literally millimeters from where he had been standing, the journey was not quick.

Upon entering Fairy Knowe, Minister Kirk saw differences in this world. The air was fresher and there was a strong scent of roses. The sun was now rising. Looking back across the field, he saw large red poppies opening their petals. In the distance, he could see a forest. To his amazement, a window opened. He was looking at his little stone church and the adjacent cemetery. His wife and children were walking into the church. He struggled mightily, but a bombardment of new laser beams latched onto him; he was in a rainbow of lights.

"God will punish you and Jesus will defend my soul," shouted the minister.

"You are in my world now," said Khalen. "Look across the poppy field through your mind's eye. They have dug a mock grave, a grave you will never occupy. They know I have your soul. Look at your family entering the church, a church where you will never again spew words of hatred calling us *sleigh maithe*."

"My family loves me," stated the minister.

"They were ashamed to find you dead at the base of this tree in your nightgown with your boots on. Your legend is now one of shame. They all wondered why a grown man shamelessly approached his enemy at night in his nightgown. What an embarrassment for humanity, to find you dead the next morning in such attire. If you cooperate with me, things could go quickly for you. This light beam can become very dense."

"I will cooperate on one condition," stated the minister. "I want to attend the christening of my first child."

"That is very interesting," said Khalen. "I will consider your request. You have reached your life's destination. Enjoy your first day in my world."

A rainbow of lights converged into a brilliant white beam and bore a hole into the fairy tree. Reverend Kirk's soul moved through the white light; it became tightly locked in near the top of the tree. The light went out. Imprisoned in total darkness, all he could do was pray.

"If you can hear me minister," said Khalen, "you should feel privileged to become our first soul; your life is not in vain for your soul will make the universe a stronger place. We good folk are a more deserving species than human folk; we are eternally grateful to you. It was unfortunate for you but fortunate for us that your heart gave way. Luck has turned in my direction. One day soon, I will find a way to make your soul my own. You are our solution for eternal life. I hope your transition will be quick and your incarceration will not be long."

CHAPTER 2

ONE CHANCE AT FREEDOM

The passage of time slowly became relevant to Minister Kirk. With each passing day, he saw a little more light and soon could tell the difference between night and day. His spirit soared when he heard the desperate scratchy scream of a baby owl below him followed by the comforting quiet response from its mother delivering a deer mouse for dinner.

Clearer sight followed sounds; Reverend Kirk could see in all directions and hear everything from the garden below. With joy, he watched a squirrel scampering across the white-stone wavy path. The mother owl delivered more food to her baby, only Kirk now recognized they were not in a nest but a landscaped birdbath.

He heard horse's hooves clearly climbing the path up the hill. A white stallion emerged carrying a lady with long flowing dark black hair and dressed in white satin, both horse and rider wearing crowns of starflowers. She dismounted and King Khalen greeted her with a kiss. Minister Kirk immediately recognized his adversary, the last person he had seen as a mortal. The couple walked hand in hand to the base of the tree, sat down and began talking.

"We are embarking on a new future, my queen," said Khalen looking into her deep blue eyes. "The legend of Khalen and Lilliana will be the greatest story ever told. I will take the minister's soul as my own. Providing there are no complications, you will then receive a soul, one of your choosing."

"I am honored with that possibility," said Lilliana. "It is our good fortune to capture him. For him to have a heart attack and then die at the optimum moment for you to harness his soul must be a sign from God. We must be the favored ones."

"I am certain of it, my dear. Capturing the soul was very easy in comparison to transferring it to our DNA. The soul is a dense nugget of energy; it is the seed of life, so strong and illusive in many ways. When I find the key to complete transference I will take the minister's soul. His is likely the strongest soul on the planet. When I accomplish this, you will be able to choose whatever soul you wish. You may want to choose an offspring of the minister."

"I see. Is it painful for the minister to be locked inside this tree?"

"He has no substantial physical presence," explained Khalen. "I have an electromagnetic hold on his essence, the seed of his existence. I believe he is losing his ability to hear and communicate. Sight would be the last sense to go. At that point I should face no resistance to adding his gene to our DNA."

"Would not that change our own identity?"

"When a person receives a new heart, he does not become the donor. During the transplant, the minister will lose his identity. He will die in the same manner that we die; simply cease to exist."

"I wish there were some other way," said Lilliana.

"There is no other way," said Khalen. "The strong survive in the universe and we are stronger than humans. The universe will be a far better place with us than with them. We are the superior species. I do understand your kindness and compassion. It is one of your strengths as a queen."

"Do you have compassion for the minister?" asked Lilliana.

"I have compassion for him. He knows I did not kill him, that his heart gave way. I have a plan to show him I am compassionate and that he can trust his soul to me. Before he completely loses his senses I am going to allow him to have his last request."

"What is that?"

"His wife has delivered a baby girl. He wants to attend the christening of his child. Although it is a slight risk, I am granting his request."

"Is there any chance he could escape?"

"My only concern is the possibility of someone using an iron weapon. Typically they do not carry knives and swords in their churches."

"What could they do?" questioned Lilliana.

"An iron blade could break the electromagnetic hold on him. There is little to no chance anything like that would happen in an area where they profess their love for each other and God."

"That still sounds risky."

"A blade would have to be tossed perfectly to break my connection. I do not believe anyone would come to his aid even if one should possess a weapon. Reports show the townspeople are still angry with him, afraid that he has put them in danger from us. On the other hand, the reward for this act of benevolence could be great. He is inviting us to a christening. We could begin a fruitful relationship with his offspring. His child's soul could become a very valuable asset, one you may consider to take as yours someday."

"The child does carry his genes. You may be right about that," agreed Lilliana. "Once you possess a soul, do you think we can achieve the same control of humans in their world that we have here?"

"That is the plan, my love. Through poets and politicians, we will make humans love us. We will infiltrate their hopes, dreams, and prayers. Their energies will work against them and be under our control. Come and watch the christening, my love. I want you to see the ritual these humans take in protecting their young. You will be amused to see the minister's grave near the church. They gave him a view in a direct line of sight to our minister's tree. Townsfolk agree with me that he got what he deserved."

A low dense fog blanketed the field between Doon Hill and the cemetery. Khalen and Lilliana escorted Minister Kirk's spirit through the fog to his church. People began to arrive and found the old church boarded up. Minister Kirk's cousin, Graham, took down the boards and opened the door for the minister's widow and baby girl, Marjorie. Standing next to them were the minister's sons, Robert E. Kirk Jr, Colin, and William. A priest followed carrying a Bible. Altogether, there were ten adults and the children. The minister stood before the congregation to start the baptism.

Khalen allowed the reverend's spirit to float above the child and mother. Everyone in the church saw the apparition and was stunned. Graham remembered his vivid dream. This was real.

"Throw the knife, Graham!" shouted the minister for everyone to hear. The small gathering cowered; they looked terrified at the sight of Kirk's ghost in his nightgown. Khalen and Lilliana were shocked and concerned. Graham was stunned; he remembered his promise to help his cousin. He pulled the knife from his belt, looked at the ghostly apparition and then at Kirk's baby girl.

"Throw the knife, Graham," shouted the desperate minister once again. Graham did not.

Without anyone's awareness, Khalen floated to stand beside the mother and child. He shouted at the minister, "Come on Kirk; beg for Graham to throw the knife. This is your only chance to save your soul."

To Margaret, Khalen whispered mockingly, "We will take Marjorie's soul in exchange for your husband's. Beg Graham to throw the knife."

Margaret looked at Graham and then at her husband. "I warned you about all of this," she furiously screamed. "I pray to God for my child's protection."

Reverend Kirk hovered above his family. He said a prayer unheard by any in the room. Lilliana motioned for Kirk to come to her and he did so; they floated out of the church and to Kirk's grave. Khalen remained with the child, studying her mind and speaking to her until the start of the christening. With one last gesture, he made the child smile, for all children have the gift of second sight for a few years. Satisfied with his plan, he then joined Lilliana and Kirk at the grave.

"Your people did not want to help you," stated Khalen. "They put this grave in a direct line of sight to your tree not to honor you, but to punish you for making us angry. Look upon this grave from atop your tree. Know that I have been more compassionate to you than your own kind. Relinquish your soul freely and end this nightmare."

"Never," replied Kirk.

They waited for the christening to end and overheard Graham as he walked out of the church with no intention of visiting the grave.

"Kirk's gone," said Graham. "His soul is lost forever. Let us hope we are not punished because of his book. God bless this child and his children. Stay clear of his grave."

Khalen and Lilliana escorted the reverend back to his home in the massive pine tree.

"He must have heard us speak about the knife," said Lilliana. "This was a much bigger risk than I expected."

"Going forward, I do not care what he hears," said Khalen. "This was his last opportunity to escape. His soul is doomed to be ours."

CHAPTER 3

Knights Templar Stand Guard

Trapped back inside the pine tree, Minister Kirk had not finished his first prayer when he received a visitor. The prospect of communicating with another individual seemed impossible, but the voice of a friendly spirit penetrated the cells of the tree.

"It looks as if you've gotten into a tight mess Minister Kirk," said the spirit. "Allow me to introduce myself. I am Hugues de Payens, the original grand master of the Knights Templar. My good friend, Godfrey de St-Omer, and I started the crusades to end religious persecution. Have you heard of us?"

"With all the mysteries of the universe and by the grace of God, I have heard of you and thank you for visiting me," replied the minister. "Your knights are considered to be the purest knights ever to take up the cause. Have you come to free me?"

"I'm so sorry, dear minister. I would love to do nothing more than that, but alas I have no power over the hold on you. We are neighbors of sorts. I guard the ninth gateway to Hell just down that path behind me. It is off to the side of this hill along with the other eight gateways. Can you see things?"

"I see and hear everything remarkably well," replied the minister. "You're a sight for sore eyes."

"There has been much chatter about you and your book," said the knight. "We, and I mean me and my other knights, were delighted in how you frightened the fairies by charging up the hill. It saddens us to see you in this situation."

"I've failed in my quest to stop these siths. They plan to use my soul as their own and doom me to a silent death, void of eternal life. I will fight them with all the will I can muster. Guarding the gates of Hell, you say?"

21

"There are nine gateways to Hell, small pinholes where evil souls spend eternity," said the knight. "This world, as you now have experienced, is parallel to the earth we both love. Nine other worlds parallel this world. All nine are realms of Hell, each one controlled by the three-headed beast, the Devil.

"When someone passes away in our world, they come into this realm and wait for their judgment. Many souls go on to the outer universe wherever God needs them. Some reach Heaven very quickly. Others, as you have warned your parishioners, pass through the gates of Hell for punishment. My eight associates, the original Knights Templar, and I are on duty from God to guard the gates of Hell, also referred to as the circles. We each stand at a gate and provide our services to God and mankind."

"It's a pleasure meeting you, sir. What service do you provide?"

"We assist souls needing to go to Hell and prevent them from leaving once they get there. You are a strong soul and must remain strong. These fairies are clever and a very determined lot. I hope they're not successful in taking your soul."

"I hope not, too. I fear humankind will lose favor with God and lose our place in the universe should that happen. What are your days like then?" questioned the minister.

"I stand at the ninth gateway, the devil's domain. I escort the most evil of all souls. The last thing our world needs is for evil spirits to work their way back home and cause more harm. As the leader of the Knights Templar, I give counsel where needed. You will meet all my knights."

"Is this your eternity then?" asked the minister.

"We knights will remain at our posts until the end of the earth or human existence on the planet. Afterward, we have been promised a home in Heaven."

"That could be a long time," posed the minister.

"Time in this parallel world is irrelevant to what you know as time. There is no true way to understand its differences. You will learn much about this world and Hell from my knights. They will enthusiastically tell their tales to you and be thrilled that you can hear and see them."

"It will truly be an honor to meet them. Have they made journeys down there?"

"Heavens no," said Hugues. "Our souls would get trapped down there. The Devil somehow feeds on souls. Recently, fairies have travelled to the depths of Hell and my knights have seen everything."

"Really, the siths have been in Hell? Why would they go down there?"

"You are the reason, my dear Minister Kirk; you've really stirred up everything. There has been a raging argument about how to handle you ever since you started writing your book. One group, the *Raptorials*, wanted you killed and the other group, the *Tolerants*, wanted your soul. Khalen, the leader of the *Tolerants*, tried to unite all of them by taking combinations of groups to Hell. He hoped to teach all of them lessons about morality, knowing that many of them would go to Hell for their behavior. In addition to *Raptorials* and *Tolerants* there are *Dissidents*, such dregs as witches and banshees that are just bad. Khalen's main objective was to convince everyone to follow him."

"There are some members of my congregation who could benefit from seeing Hell," mused the minister.

"Most people could, I dare say," added the knight. "In any event, fairies discovered the parallel worlds of Hell. They took journeys into the circles providing their own light that gave us a view. We were all finally able to see clearly what's down there; it's become so polluted over the ages since the time Dante first reported it and I first came here."

"That's fascinating," said the minister.

"Prior to the fairies discovery," the knight continued, "I was the only one who had ever seen Hell. In the past it was quite different; it was smaller and light filtered easily between the realms although it got darker as one descended. Recently we could see nothing with the exception of distant firelight. Fairy folk are very clever in how they pass between worlds and how they can make their own light."

"All of my knights love to talk about what they've seen. They try to tell their tales to good souls passing through this world, but they do not stay long enough. We are getting busier and busier as our world becomes more and more evil. My knights will be quick in telling their tales for they have a lot to do."

"Fair folk journeying to Hell?" questioned Kirk with wonder in his voice. "Why didn't the devil keep them? They are pure evil."

"Unfortunately, they have no soul and are no use to Satan," said Hugues. "They are superior to us in many ways but totally useless to the devil."

"I've heard their argument about being superior," said the minister.

"I must admit, they do have some good qualities," said Hugues. "They're not murderers, but they do steal babies, and that would surely land them in hell one day."

"I had that very conversation with the fairy king," said Kirk. "He believes God will forgive him once he has a soul."

FALIAS

In the frost-grown city of Falias, it's said that ravens fly like old banners of wars. Snow white ravens amid the ice-green spires. The oldest city on the planet and built from granites and gems.

"You're talking about Khalen, of course," said the knight. He is a 'picasso' in my book. The other leaders of this world don't like him much."

"Who are they?" asked Kirk.

"There are four major cities and regions," explained the knight. "Khalen leads the northern city, Falias, the oldest city on the planet and built from granite and gems. His political party is the *Tolerants*, the group that did not want you killed. Khalen wants to steal our hearts and minds before taking the soul. He does not want people to be afraid of him but to love him."

"I see; he wants the souls of folk who love him."

"That's correct. The other leaders belong to the party of the *Raptorials*. They have been the aggressive ones, intimidating folk to stop them from doing what you've been doing."

"Their strategy is working. Everyone's afraid of them."

"The disagreement on how to handle you in particular has reached a feverish pitch. They were so afraid of your weapon, the iron knife you left behind. I saw the whole thing. You were brilliant in your strategy. Even though they magically change into a mist, fairies are terrified of ghosts. It was a shame you didn't use your knife."

"I had a heart attack. You said there were four cities. Khalen seems to be outnumbered. Who are the other leaders?"

"In the west, Lady Vivienne presides over Murias, a city built over the ocean. To the south is Finias, an oasis city in the desert protected by a blue dome and led by the sun goddess Brighid. To the east, there is Gorias, the city of air, constructed between two mountains and led by King Odin."

"Khalen lives in his palace at Fairy Knowe, and rules the granite city of Falias, the most ancient city in both worlds. I could talk all day, but I have some business to attend. The Ninth circle of Hell gets the most evil ones. I know you understand."

"I've heard of Brighid, Odin, and Lady Vivienne. They are legendary."

ᴐ☙ 𝔍INIAS ☙ᴐ

It is well-known that people here are warm-hearted, that light is perpetual and night never descends.

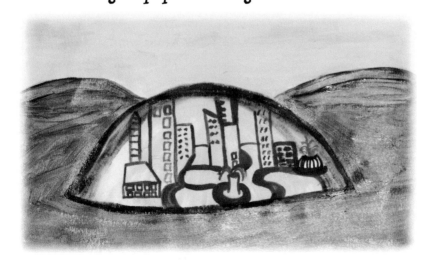

GORIAS
The mountains of Gorias inspire deep thoughts and high intellect, cutting through ignorance to clarity.

"Their legends have touched many; most people did not realize they were fairies. This species live on and on; they die only when they give up on life. Pixies are the oldest of them. Dwarves, elves, gnomes, leprechauns, and selkies are just to name a few. There are bad ones like witches, banshees, goblins and others. I could go on, but I must return to my post."

"Thank you for visiting me," said the minister. "I've studied many of them. I would like the other knights to tell me their tales. I want to hear more from you too, and all about this world."

MURIAS

In Murias, it is understood that you must open your heart to your own feelings and the feelings of others.

"I'll see that it's done," reassured Hugues. "My knights are going to love talking to you. To have a captive audience will be a treat for them. I am sorry I said that. They would be eager to tell you our tales, providing that you are here long enough. I am sorry I said that, too. It's been a long time since my last conversation."

"I understand; no apology is needed," said the minister. "I'm sorry I've delayed you. I love to keep my congregation as long as possible and I would love for you to stay."

"Circle Nine is the deepest part of Hell," said Hugues proudly. The devil is a three-headed beast and rules the nine realms from his domain of fire and ice. Thanks to the fairy queen, I saw him, all three evil faces. You are a strong soul and must remain strong. Show God He was right to give man the gift of eternal life. Jesus will defend your soul; you can count on that. I must return to my post."

"I'll look forward to your tale," said the minister as the knight floated away.

CHAPTER 4

Knights Start
Their Tales

In no time, the minister received his second visitor.

"Hello Minister Kirk, I'm Godfrey de Saint-Omer, second in command. Are you really locked up in this tree?"

"Unfortunately, it's true," replied the minister. "Thank you for visiting me. It is my honor to meet you. Thank you for defending religious freedom."

"I'm pleased to meet you; you flatter me," said the knight. "I'm sorry we can't help you escape. It is an honor for me to speak to a man of the cloth and thank you for your service to God. I must tell my tale quickly; I can't get behind in my duties."

"I understand," said the minister. "Carry on with your story. I will not interrupt. Perhaps we can speak more at some other time."

"We will speak often. I guard the gateway at Circle One, the first gateway to Hell. Like the other knights, I will tell you about the fairies and their journey into my circle. It is a joy to know I make them uneasy. They ignored me for centuries until they discovered what I do. It is ironic they want a soul but are afraid of us. They think they know everything. It's amusing to see them frightened about what they don't know."

"I tried to trick them into believing I was a ghost; it only got me here."

"It was a good strategy just the same," stated Godfrey. "You were unfortunate, but we must keep the faith. Fairies are a very clever bunch. I must proceed with my story."

"Of course, my dear fellow, please proceed."

"Queen Lilliana discovered Circle Nine when she became curious and followed a difficult transfer, a tough customer if you know what I mean."

"A really bad one I presume," said the minister.

"You know the type. Hugues will tell you about that. My tale is about Circle One. Hugues saw these worlds long ago when light penetrated the circles. Through a dream, he made a connection with Dante Alighieri, the poet, and passed along the information about Hell. The poet delivered his message. Have you read his poem?"

"I did read it and it seemed so real. I am now anxious to see how it has changed. Go on with your story."

"I'm concerned about the state of humanity. Circle One has grown to be the largest of the devil's realms and is still growing. The ones I send down there cared nothing about their soul. This is my tale.

> I was standing guard in heavy fog when the mist began to lift. During the night, fair folk had carved a number '1' into a head stone by the circle and had built a path connecting all the circles to the garden underneath this tree.
>
> Through the mist, I saw Queen Lilliana riding up the main path, the path you used all the time. She dismounted her white stallion and came down our path, a path the fairies created to link each gateway or circle. The queen came to my circle and took a seat. She was so beautiful with deep blue eyes and silky black hair. Khalen soon came walking out of the fog from the direction of the other circles and greeted her. They sat together and started talking.
>
> 'Does the sulfur from Circle Nine still make you dizzy?' asked Khalen.
>
> 'My dizziness has lessened a bit,' she replied.
>
> 'I know you want to go inside the other circles,' said Khalen, 'but I do not think you should take another journey.'
>
> 'I will be fine. I have seen the worst. It may take a little time to recover, but a little dizziness will not stop me. The Knight at Circle Nine told me that we would be punished and sent to one of the circles if we steal the human soul.'

'God will forgive us,' said Khalen. 'There is no eternity without a soul. We have to take the chance. With no soul, we are doomed. I am sure many Tolerants will end up there. Their terrorism will lead them to punishment. Dissidents, especially witches and banshees, will find a place down there.'

'If only we could capture Kirk, we could stop all this hostility,' stated Lilliana.

"They talked about you all the time, Reverend," added Godfrey.

'We will capture him one day,' said Khalen, 'for I have a plan. His soul is strong and he will serve us well. Your discovery of Hell will help unite Raptorials and Dissidents with us. One day we will all be Tolerants. Dissidents and Raptorials will take turns going to the different circles. Their experience will make them see things our way."

'I am anxious to get started,' said Lilliana.

'Today a witch will go with you and Honey Driftsfur. Regina Spideroaster has a loud voice and news of her experience will spread quickly.'

'I hope these missions work to unite us,' said Lilliana.

'It is my hope, as well,' agreed Khalen. 'I've been studying how the Devil operates. Our population really needs to know the negative consequences of having a soul.'

'Once we show them the evidence,' stated Lilliana, 'no one would take the risk of spending eternity down there.'

Suddenly a screech from the mother owl living in this tree resonated all over the hill. She had swooped down from her perch to protect her baby from the witch, Regina Spideroaster, who had come through the fog with Honey Driftsfur, one of Khalen's elite guards. The mother owl flew from the baby owl's birdbath directly at Regina; with her claws, she grabbed the witch's hat and a small clump of her thinning hair. The witch screamed and cursed at the owl.

'The mother owl is only protecting her baby,' scolded Honey, her green eyes flashing as she shook her hair, the color of honey and her namesake. 'Do not curse at her.'

'She snatched some of my hair,' shouted the witch, showing her a few of the black and gray strands.

'I am sorry,' said Honey. 'I will make you a new hat from purple and yellow tulips when we get back from Circle One.'

'Wouldn't that be sweet,' mocked Regina. 'I'll make you some pixie pears with sweet milk and hope it makes you puke.'

'Let us try to get along,' said Khalen now joining them with Lilliana at his side. 'The owl knows you could eat her baby, Regina. You frightened her. I hope this little incident does not give you a bad attitude. This is a serious journey and we need to work together.'

'Rats scratching and dung beetles,' said Regina. 'I get what little hair I have pulled out and then told to have a good attitude with red and yellow tulips. Let's get this party started so I can get on with my life.'

'We are going to a stale, musty world,' continued Khalen. 'This journey should not be too long. From what I can see there is a lot of nothing down there.'

They left the garden with Regina trying to sort out her hair and followed the path to stand before me.

I said to them, 'A lot of nothing down there is an understatement.' They ignored me and pretended I was not there. It gives me joy to make them feel uncomfortable.

'Hell sounds delightful,' said Regina.

'I have read a poem about Circle One,' offered Honey. 'It's supposed to be full of light, fresh air and beautiful villas.'

'Perhaps that was true in times past,' said Khalen. 'From what I can tell, light filters down through the circles; each circle receives less and less light every day.'

I stepped out from my position to stand before them; they backed off. I felt compelled to tell them this: 'Circle One began to clog up as men gained in intelligence. Poets claimed the soul was nothing more than a dream. Those who believed the poets followed their thinking and found their way here. The negative energy from their souls now blocks the sunlight. In these times, light filters up from the fires in Circle Nine. Beware; you may have a problem finding your way out.' "I stepped back to my position."

'We are not going to have the same problems as your species,' said Khalen. 'We are smarter than you.'

'That damn owl stole my hat,' said Regina. 'I can't believe you're talking to a damn ghost. I can't go to Hell without a hat.'

'You will not need a hat for the journey,' said Khalen.

'You would not be here had you not helped Baba Yaga to steal the baby Maggie O'Malley,' said Honey. 'That baby could have died. I have given her a good home. My cousin, Moth Beamfrost, has provided her a fine life in Gorias.'

'You made no effort to send the baby back to her family,' retorted Regina. 'You're just as bad as us.'

'There is no hope for Baba Yaga,' said Khalen. 'There is a little hope for you so long as you understand what you are about to experience. Lilliana and Honey will help you if you stay focused.'

Lilliana took Regina and Honey by the hand and formed a circle. They began to spin, became a mist, and went into the circle. I looked in and smelled the thick, musty smell, but there was light around them. They found the air was muddy with giant earthworms slithering around them. Regina let out a soft cackle as if she was enjoying it. They travelled through this wormhole and landed on a dirt floor stirring up the smell even more. Breaking their circle and with Lilliana leading the way, they followed a dirt path that led them into a group of dead trees full of dead leaves that had not fallen. Beside and behind each tree I could see souls. Some moved slowly and some stood still.

'What's their problem?' asked Regina.

'They did not believe they had a soul,' said Lilliana. 'They are receiving what they expected in death. Many were so lazy, and dependent on others; they gave up their free will. They are harmless; there is nothing to them.'

'They're boring,' said Regina. 'Perhaps I could try a magic trick to liven the place up.'

'It would not interest them,' said Lilliana. 'They do not believe in magic. They do not believe in anything.'

'Do they believe they are here?' asked Honey.

'That is a good question,' replied Lilliana. 'I will find out. Excuse me sir, where are we?'

'I'm neither here nor there,' said the man.

'Do you remember your family?' asked Honey

'My family is somewhere, but we were just biology.'

'What was your understanding of life?' asked Honey.

'I believe in science. This place does not exist. I'm in a bad dream.'

'Science cannot teach you what it does not know,' countered Honey.

'That's when I believed in my government. They took care of me.'

'Your government cannot take care of you now.' explained Honey. 'Your soul was your responsibility.'

'The church invented the soul to get money,' said another. 'Everyone knows that.'

'Is your family here?' asked Regina. 'Have you looked for them?'

'Why should I? This dream will be over soon, and then I can sleep.'

Regina danced around a man cackling, laughing, and chanting a spell. 'You are now a chicken,' she commanded and lifted her hands to cast magic dust on the soul.

'Why?' asked the man and nothing happened.

'I was trying to lift your spirits,' said Regina.

'I have no spirit. You're ridiculous.'

A giant earthworm slithered by and carried the soul away on its back.

'Regina, that was so nice of you to try to lift his spirits,' complimented Honey. 'You could have helped him to free his mind and better understand the unknown.'

'Whatever you say Ms. Pretty Honey Pie,' said Regina. 'I'd rather push your buttons than be here with these boring souls. Lilliana, is there anything else to see?'

'No,' said Lilliana, 'let us leave here. I have seen enough. This is a waste land.'

Reforming their circle, they slowly ascended in the musty air, back through the muddy wormhole that clogged the pinhole of Circle 1. With a slight pop, they re-entered Fairy Knowe. They were filthy, smelled awful, and ran past Khalen looking like they were going to puke.

"That's my tale," said Godfrey. "I've got to get back to my position. Things in Hell have changed for the worse since Dante Alighieri. You know he did not take credit for having a great imagination; he gave credit to God for his inspiration. God actually had Hugues de Payens (our grand master) deliver the inspiration through dreams. Your next visitor will be from Circle Two. His name is Payne de Monteverdi, a relative to Hugues."

"Thank you for the story, kind sir," said the minister, "and thank you for your service."

"I look forward to sharing another tale with you. It is about a holy relic, the Holy Nail. Take care, my friend."

CHAPTER 5

LUST & FAIR FOLK IN CIRCLE TWO

7

ncapsulated in the massive pine tree, the beleaguered minister spent the bulk of his time praying. Khalen and Lilliana often came to the garden below him, planning a festival, or just relaxing. For the most part, he observed gentle beings, appreciating everything in nature. Their celebrations continued through every kind of weather, given their true purpose on earth as caretakers.

What the minister was unable to see was how their happiness had changed when God gave humans a soul. From that moment, a generally sad expression settled in on their faces, even in moments of joy. They have never come to grips with how God gave an inferior species the opportunity for eternal life after all they had done for the earth.

Minister Kirk understood this jealousy and melancholy. He was a compassionate person and prayed for a solution to end the conflict. He knew it was God's will to test souls. The universe was beyond massive and He alone fully understood the battle between good vs. evil.

Still, the melancholy of the fairies made him constantly think of his own sadness. He often felt like a seedling trapped inside a cone. Comforting memories about his family and congregation always lifted his spirits. Believing that he would survive and see his family in Heaven gave him strength. He knew this concept was foreign to his enemy.

Days and seasons passed by differently in each world yet time seemed to stand still. One day, with the rain pouring and the thunder booming in both worlds, his second visitor arrived.

"Good morning," announced a knight rather briskly. "I am Payne de Monteverdi, the knight who guards the gateway to Circle Two. Lust is the issue down there. As you can well understand, I am always very busy. This wonderful break in the weather has given me a few moments to tell my tale. I will get right to it for the rain and thunder are but brief distractions to my sinners. I have been looking to share this with you for a long time. I feel awful about your incarceration."

"Carry on," said the minister. "I understand the breadth of your expertise."

"I must say, I was a ladies man in my time and no doubt was chosen to guard this circle for that reason. I loved and respected the ladies, every one of them, and they loved me. Knights have great passion; great passion deserves mutual respect of the highest honor. Very well then, here's my tale."

It was a snowy winter's day. I was conversing with my relative, Knight Archambaud de St. Agnan. I heard two fairy guards, Petal

Hailfrost and Honey Driftsfur, attending to the young owl in the fairy garden. Through the trees, I saw their queen, Lilliana, riding up the main path. She sat proudly on her white stallion, wearing a long white cape, a white fur hood that contrasted with her silky black hair. She looked magnificent with large snowflakes gently glancing from her eyelashes.

A few moments later, I saw Thorn Cornembers, a loyal Tolerant true to his name (a thorn in the side of anyone opposed to Khalen) with Olive Flametree (a rebellious Raptorial) holding hands. Olive was in custody for inciting witches. She did not look like a prisoner, pretty with a soft olive complexion (hence her name), and very proud like a warrior princess. She was wearing the colors of the rainbow with her hair to match. Each fingernail was a different color.

'I am sorry you lost your cosmetic case during your arrest at the protest,' said Thorn. 'You were quite a handful.'

'No worries,' replied Olive, 'I am surprised, yet flattered. You remembered that amidst all the worms.'

'You gave an impressive demonstration,' said Thorn with a smile. 'I love your passion.'

'I have always been fighting for some cause,' she said.

'I hope our journey to Hell brings our folk some peace,' stated Thorn. 'We should be able to solve our differences with love and respect.'

'Sometimes fighting is the only way to get things changed,' offered Olive.

'Fighting is the result of losing the will to compromise,' said Thorn looking deep into her eyes.

'You are a deep thinker,' she said with a smile. 'Would you ever put passion before your duties?'

'I would rather die than shirk my duties,' he replied. 'My job on this mission is to protect you. I will do just that.'

'I am glad you want to protect me; thanks for not putting me in handcuffs.'

'Holding your hand is much better,' he said finally returning her smile with one of his own.

'That is fine,' she said while putting her hand on his shoulder. 'Do not get any ideas about us. You are not my type.'

They strolled to the landscaped birdbath in the Fairy Garden to join the others.

'I am happy to see both of you civil today,' said Lilliana. 'Holding hands like friends is refreshing. We are going into Circle Two where lustful humans are punished for inappropriate behavior. We need to be on our guard for trickery. What questions do you have?'

'Do you think I am bad because I do not like straight-laced lads like Thorn?' asked Olive.

'You know very little about Thorn,' said Lilliana. 'I think you are wrong for prejudging him before you know him. When he is on your side, he is passionate about defending you. You and he could become best of friends. Perhaps you should get to know him better.'

'Spiked hair and no sideburns? He is dull and boring,' stated Olive. 'Let us get on with this.'

'There is a knight standing by the circle,' explained Lilliana. 'He is ghastly, but do not be concerned. There is one at every circle and they are too busy to cause us any harm.'

I took offense to the ghastly part, continued Payne. I was a handsome knight in my day and highly appreciated by all the ladies. I put them on the highest pedestal.

"You're doing fine with the female voices, by the way," commented Minister Kirk.

"Thank you, I think." said the knight.

The fairies walked to Circle Two. Lilliana took the free hand of Thorn and Olive to form a circle. They began to spin, and on the seventh spin, Liliana shouted 'Reverse!' They became a rainbow mist and entered the gateway.

It was a tunnel with heavy smoke and sickening sweet perfume. I could tell that much without light. When the fairies descended into the circle, I could see swirls of deep pink and red smoke closing in on them. They landed in the corner of a room with dim blue and red lights. Souls were mingling with each other. I heard music, but there was no song; that is, the music kept repeating and repeating never reaching a melody. From across the room a soldier, who surprisingly looked like Khalen, was talking to a woman; he looked directly at Lilliana and stared.

Her jaw dropped.

'Excuse me,' she said to Olive and Thorn, 'I will be right back.'

Olive and Thorn watched from the corner of the smoky room as the soldier, who looked like Khalen, exited with Lilliana following him.

A man and woman talking and cuddling in a nearby booth captured Olive's attention; she nudged Thorn to look at them.

'You are the most powerful man in the world,' said the woman. 'I am so privileged that you find me beautiful.'

'You are the future of our country,' he said gazing into her eyes. 'With a beautiful face, a beautiful body, and a beautiful mind, you're all that any man would want.'

'What about your wife?' asked the young woman?

'I once felt this way for her, but we never - I want to feel that way again.'

He took the young woman in his arms and started to kiss her. A fire started at their feet and slowly spread upwards; the flames from their passion consumed the two of them. Within a short while, there was nothing but smoke where they stood.

'Let's give them a hand,' said a loud voice.

Cheers filled the room, continued Payne. After a few minutes, we heard the same two people talking; they repeated the same scene. A group of women slowly gathered around Thorn. They put their hands in his hair and on his leather jacket. Two of them nudged Olive away and pulled Thorn to the dance floor.

A loud voice announced, 'Look ladies, he's so strong and he's not catching on fire. He's a gift from the master. Come dance with him.'

Thorn enjoyed the attention. Olive had a puzzled look about her.

'What should I do then?' she asked.

'Lilliana will be along any minute,' said Thorn. 'Take a seat at the corner table.'

Each of the women took turns dancing with Thorn until one of them got jealous and started a fight. Thorn slipped away from them and returned to sit with Olive. Several women forgot completely about Thorn; they became locked in a struggle, pulling each other's hair. There was no effort from anyone to stop them. Pulling hair escalated to scratching eyes badly enough to deform their faces. They fought until they were set on fire. Meanwhile, the crowd at the tables continued talking like nothing was happening.

'I thought you were a good boy,' said Olive after the ordeal was over.

'I am good,' said Thorn. 'I was only dancing.'

'Your dance is wicked,' said Olive, 'but in a good way.'

'I think you are starting to like me,' claimed Thorn.

'Do you like me?' asked Olive pouting her lips.

'I like you. I disagree with you, but there is a lot to like about you.'

'Name one thing,' said Olive brushing back her hair.

'I love the way you inspire people. You are very passionate about what you believe in. You could put your talent to a better purpose.'

'I cannot believe it,' said Olive.

'Please believe me,' pleaded Thorn.

'I do not mean that. I do believe you. I cannot believe me.'

'What do you mean?'

'I have been unable to find a bad boy back home, and now I find a good one that I like, and we are in Hell.'

She leaned close to Thorn and kissed him on the mouth. The two were so much into each other they did not see Lilliana coming.

'Look at this cozy scene,' remarked Lilliana. 'What are you two doing?'

'We are waiting for you,' said Olive, 'and getting to know each other better like you suggested. Was that King Khalen?'

'That must have been a mirage. I went outside the building and the image vaporized. We have to get out of here. Our mission is over.'

'Why?''' asked Thorn and Olive speaking simultaneously.

'You two look like you are falling in love. There is no love in Hell,' scolded the queen. 'You could start some chain of events that could cause this whole demented circle to explode. Take my hands. We are leaving now, and I mean now!'

They joined hands in a circle and travelled back through the smoky, perfumed, pink, and red tunnel. I was sweating a little when they returned and steam was rising off the stones surrounding the circle. There was a flash of light and Lilliana appeared beside me. Suddenly the steaminess changed back to snow blowing around in a whirlwind. There was another flash of light; Olive and Thorn appeared smiling and holding hands.

"That's it," said Payne. "That's my tale. What do you think?"

"I must say you Knights are quite good story tellers."

"Thank you, kind sir. Did Godfrey tell you his tale of the Holy Nail?"

"He plans to tell it to me."

"It's a wonderful tale," stated Payne. "An ancestor of mine guards the relic to this day. Your next visitor will be along shortly. He's quite a talker;

got his skills, no doubt, from enjoying the fruit of the vine. He keeps me on my toes. Farewell for now."

Payne de Monteverdi turned to float away and bumped into Archambaud de St. Agnan, the next knight scheduled to visit the tree.

"Excuse me," said Archambaud, "I thought you were never going to finish."

"Did the fairies see you coming?" asked Payne.

"I'm not sure," replied his friend. "Why do you ask?"

"I don't think we should be here together. Fairies may think we're conspiring against them and retaliate on the minister."

"You're right," agreed Archambaud. "I've been too eager to tell my tale. Share your thoughts with the other knights."

Payne de Monteverdi passed over Khalen and Lilliana on his way back to Circle Two, making eye contact with the king. Khalen looked at him and then at Archambaud at top of the tree. The king showed no sign of being concerned.

CHAPTER 6

A Tale of Gluttony in Circle Three

ood day, my reverend, I am Archambaud de St. Agnan. Gluttony in our world is growing, be it food or drink. Circle Three is becoming as bad as One and Two. I can't tarry; this weather may soon change."

"Good day to you, monsieur," returned the minister. "I'm very appreciative of the weather and a good tale. Did you perhaps obsess on food or drink during your days on earth?"

"Everyone knew I enjoyed the fruit of the vine. Obsessing on it is a bit of a stretch. Why do you ask?"

"It could make you an expert on the subject. I greatly admire the reputation of the Templars. Please carry on."

"I can only imagine the taste of a fine port while telling my story. It was a morning like this when I watched the fairies go into Hell. I remember shouting to Payne, 'lustful drunkards are difficult to handle on days like this.' He deals with similar problems, you know. I'm so sorry to hear about your incarceration, but am happy to meet you."

"It's nice of you to visit me," said the minister. "Tales on a day like this are wonderful. I often read the Bible to my boys on days like this, especially the story of the Great Flood. I, like you, enjoy a good port wine from time to time."

"You are a good soul. It's a shame you didn't get more support in your search for the fairy folk. The sound of rain helps to heal our disappointments," said Archambaud. "I must be quick with my tale."

"I understand; you've much work to do."

On that enlightening day it was raining. Regina Spideroaster, the witch, was the first to arrive. She was cursing at the rain and carrying mushrooms and herbs she had gathered from the woods.

King Khalen rode up behind her on his black horse. He seemed to enjoy the rain hitting him in the face, and called out, 'Regina, what are you doing here?'

'I'm not causing any problems,' she said. 'I want to see the rats and bugs.'

'This is not an amusement park,' scolded Khalen. 'These circles are real places. If you should ever get a soul, you would end up in one of these circles for eternity or close to eternity. In this Circle Three, the Devil deals with gluttony, something witches are guilty of.'

'We all have our weaknesses,' said Regina. 'I brought some herbs and mushrooms to make you all a good beverage. This rain is awful and that musty first circle was depressing.'

'Are you becoming nicer Regina?' asked Khalen.

'I must admit, Circle One made me think a bit,' replied the witch.

Walking up the main path to join them was Petal Hailfrost, Honey Driftsfur, Beetle Willowleaf, and Chestnut Silvertwist.

'Good morning all,' said Khalen. 'Petal, Honey, why are you here on such a rainy morning? Beetle and Chestnut are taking the journey with me.'

'We are going to turtle sit for Beetle and Chestnut,' said Petal. 'Their turtles, Franklin and Ferdinand, need to be looked after while the boys are in hell.'

'We brought our turtles,' said Beetle.

'I have a sea turtle,' boasted Chestnut. 'He loves the rain. He will definitely win today.'

"*Behind them rode Lilliana on her white horse. She wore a white hooded rain jacket that glistened from the rain in the faint light of morning.*"

'It is surprising to see so many of you here,' she said. 'You could be enjoying that extra pleasant snooze you get on a rainy morning. Petal, the beautiful frost on your hair is frizzy.'

'We are turtle-sitting and a bit curious,' said Petal, taking a blue scarf that matched her eyes and covering her hair. 'You have opened

our eyes to a larger world. The last journey was so awful. We decided to try to make it fun.'

'You do have our best interests at heart,' said Lilliana.

'We can have a little fun even though you Tolerants are usually wrong about everything,' said Chestnut.

'Chestnut, I appreciate your attitude,' said Khalen. 'Before we make the human soul our own, we need to make certain everyone understands the risks.'

'Here are some little cakes and cookies with melted acorn butter for the send-off,' said Honey. 'I have plenty to share, but it is raining too hard to enjoy them.'

'I picked some wonderful mushrooms and herbs for a beverage,' said Regina.

'I brought a tent canopy for the turtle race,' said Beetle. "We can set it up for protection and then have the cakes, cookies, and beverage. Will that be okay King Khalen?'

'We will see,' said Khalen. 'An appetite may be difficult to find after we finish our business here.'

Beetle and Chestnut quickly set up the tent canopy. Beetle gave his turtle to Petal to hold and Chestnut gave his turtle to Honey. They walked with Khalen to Circle Three. Chestnut (the Raptorial), and Beetle (Khalen's guard), joined hands with Khalen in a circle. The rest of the fairy folk counted seven spins.

Lilliana shouted, 'Reverse!'

They entered the gateway; I saw them drop like heavy weights in a spinning tunnel. Prior to that, I never saw anything. Swirls of bright red and white light circled them; they dropped at dizzying speeds; it really made me dizzy.

Archambaud paused for the first time. He took a deep breath before he rushed on with his story.

They landed in a shadowy room, separated from each other with light shining on their faces. Whatever they were standing on began to tilt. It was puzzling but then I realized they were on a cattle trough. Their eyes were big and cheeks swelled; they looked as if they were going to toss their cookies. The room started to spin. Chestnut was near the bottom of the incline and fell to his knees; Beetle did the same. They were sliding ever so slowly downward. Something mushy and smelly was moving past their feet.

'What is this stuff at our feet?' asked Chestnut.

'It looks like seaweed,' said Beetle. 'It smells awful.'

'Rotten food is fermenting in alcohol,' explained Khalen, 'and it is moving us down this channel.'

'I am going to be sick,' moaned Chestnut.

'Look down there, in the shadows,' said Khalen. 'This mixture is being funneled to souls taking their turn in a food line. We are sliding toward them.'

'Why are they eating this putrid mush?' asked Chestnut.

'They are gluttons,' said Khalen. 'In life they obsessed on food, alcohol, drugs, and even work. 'They took no time for their souls. Their reward for eternity is a constant stream of food, alcohol, and drugs.'

"One soul overheard Khalen and shouted, 'I had a disease. It was not my fault.'

'I was told you could earn your way back to Circle One, said Khalen and eventually out of here.'

'I spent time in Circle One already. I did not like it there. At least here I get my fix.'

He consumed the mush.

'They have no will to help themselves. I have seen enough down here,' stated Khalen.

'I hope this smell comes out of my clothing,' said Chestnut.

They left Circle Three in a straight line floating back through the dizzy chamber. Only this time they spun in the opposite direction. Khalen popped out of the circle first followed by Beetle then Chestnut. They all staggered to the tent canopy where everyone was waiting for them.

The group was underneath the tent enjoying toadstool cakes and a bowl of mushroom broth with herbs. They laughed when Beetle fell over in the pouring rain. He was exhausted and just lay there in a puddle. Chestnut then tripped over Beetle and fell in the mud too. Both were a filthy mess and slid over each other a few times trying to get to their feet. I appreciated the humor.

'There is plenty of food and drink,' said Lilliana. 'Let us celebrate and watch the turtles. Petal has made a cake. Honey made more cookies and Regina made a mushroom beverage. What do you say fellows?'

'Did you say mushrooms?' asked Beetle. 'I have no room for mush and will never look at food and drink in the same way.'

Chestnut puked his guts out. Needless to say, they dispensed with the party.

"That's Circle Three for you," concluded Archambaud. "I'm glad I no longer have an appetite for food or drink. Nourishment for my soul is serving God. How do you feel?"

"Fair folk can be humorous, but ultimately, I've always been sickened by them," said the minister. "They've consumed the essence from our food and drink. I only wish they had consumed some of the mush. Thank you for your company and enlightening me. You told your tale well."

"Have the fairies caused you pain?" asked Archambaud de St. Agnan with great compassion.

"Aside from feeling closed in, I've blocked out anything else," said Kirk. "Memories and prayers keep me going, along with these tales of course."

"You are a strong seed," said the knight. "We'll speak again; the gluttons are waiting for me."

Just as the knight floated away, a penetrating light began working its way through the cells of the tree. It changed to many shades of red, carrying some heat with deep pulsations of sound waves. The minister initially enjoyed the soothing nature of the wave, but became cautious; to enjoy the process could be fatal. He focused his thoughts on the image of a seed, starting with a lettuce seed so small that it was a dot. The seed in his mind grew stronger like an impenetrable shell. The wave attack finally ended; Khalen's attempt to send a message to punish the minister for communicating with the knights had failed.

Minister Kirk relaxed; thoughts about his life lead him to one conclusion. His ministry had prepared him for moments like this. He felt proud to have served his congregation and proud that he made it possible for people to read the Bible. Despite his captivity, he was still interested in the fairies, wishing only that he could make notes of everything. Hatred never entered his mind. He believed in himself and was confident that Khalen had selected the wrong soul to steal.

CHAPTER 7

A Leprechaun in Hell

I t was not very long before another very concerned knight, Hugh, Count of Champagne, came to the tree.

"Good day," said the knight, "but then again I understand you're not having such a good day. Whatever just happened in this tree was very intense. Are you really in there?"

"No worries, my friend," said the minister, "God has prepared me for whatever comes my way. One day when we're in heaven, we'll laugh about this."

"We very much admire your strength. I am Count Hugh from the region of Champagne. I would love to cheer you up with a tale; but then again, could a tale about the fairies in Hell cheer you up? I'm sure you despise Hell and fairies."

"No worries again, my friend," said the minister, "Your company cheers me up and I want to know all about the fairies and Hell. In a way it's delightful to think of them down there."

"I'm glad you're the minister type," said Hugh, Count of Champagne. "In my time, I was richer than the King of France. I learned proper values, that money can do great things as long as you have a good soul. If anyone can beat these fairies, it would be you. Let me get to my tale of greed. I'm sure you know how busy we all are."

"Carry on, my good Count."

King Khalen and Queen Lilliana stood with Petal Hailfrost, one of Khalen's guards (a Tolerant), and

Sneaky McLittle (a Raptorial leprechaun) who was arrested for profiting from protests against Khalen.

'Petal Hailfrost, Sneaky McLittle,' commanded Khalen, 'please step forward. You will go with me today into Circle Four. Sneaky, your community will receive you back upon completion of your two missions. Like the others, you will be free to tell your story about the soul. These journeys to Hell are on record for everyone to see. Everyone will know the possibility of eternity in Hell should they choose not to follow the code.'

'Once we take possession of the soul,' explained Lilliana, 'Fair folk everywhere will begin the process to obtain eternal life. Breaking certain rules would lead to eternal damnation. We would be required to follow the rules of God in His universe.'

'Sneaky your arrests have involved greed and fraud,' stated the King. 'You have made a huge profit from the war. This sort of behavior would get you to Hell. I think you will learn a lot today.'

The leprechaun fidgeted like a child, though he looked like an old man.

The leprechaun fidgeted like a child, though he looked like an old man.

They walked to Circle Four. I gave them one of those looks, kind of like this with my nose scrunched up. Can you see me?

I see you; I know that look, replied the minister.

The fairies shuddered and held hands to form their circle as they always do when entering a gateway.

'Have you washed your hands today, Sneaky?' asked Petal.

'No, I've not had any money to handle,' replied the leprechaun.

'That is not funny. You are such a child. I am not going to Hell with you until you wash your hands.'

'I clean up well,' said Sneaky, touching his gold tooth with a click.

'Do not be stupid. You just put your dirty hand in your mouth. Here is a sanitized napkin. Wash your hands or I just might let you go off on your own once we are in the tunnel.'

'What should we do if something causes our circle to break?' asked Sneaky, while washing his hands.

'You look like you are afraid, Sneaky McLittle,' said Khalen. 'This is going to be fun.'

'How do you know we're going to be able to get back through this small hole?' asked Sneaky.

'I am not worried like you should be,' teased Petal.

'We leprechauns are not as bad as dwarves. Don't come asking me for money later on,' retorted Sneaky.

'Your money is dirty like your hands. Have you always been sneaky even when you were little, Sneaky?' questioned Petal.

'My father was Filch McLittle; he wanted me to be like him. Aren't you a little afraid?'

'Fear is an adventure for me,' stated Petal. 'Thanks for washing up. I will hold your hand now. So long as you do not try anything sneaky with me, you will not have anything to fear.

'Well, okay then,' said Khalen, 'If you should lose grip with us, Sneaky, just hope the souls in this realm do not want to keep you.'

'Let us do this,' said Petal.

'I'm not afraid,' said the leprechaun.

They went into their spin, became an orange vapor, and entered the gateway to Circle Four. To my surprise, I was still able to see the orange vapor until they materialized. Sneaky held Petal's hand with a death grip. They were in a tunnel of brilliant sparkling gold.

Sneaky commented, 'We must be near the end of the rainbow, the brilliance of gold.'

The glittering gold became so bright that I closed my eyes for a moment. Heat came from the circle and it got hotter and hotter. They finally broke through the tunnel; the bright gold was gone. A light supplied by the fairies showed them floating in the cavernous space where the greedy go. They drifted toward a yellowish orange glow. As they got closer, a rounded hill much like Fairy Knowe came into view. Souls were busy at work.

'This is not what I expected,' stated Sneaky McLittle. 'These souls are mining gold at the base of the hill; there's so much of it; look at the glow coming out of the mine. Look how hard they're working.'

'They are slaves, and they are mining fool's gold,' said Khalen. 'I have been studying them for a while. Look at their faces.'

'They look confused,' said Sneaky.

'It looks they are making coins at the top of the hill,' said Petal.

'They are making useless money for their master's pleasure,' explained Khalen. 'There is nothing here for them to buy. The fake money gives them nothing but frustration.'

'Look on the other side of the hill,' said Petal. 'Another group is busy melting the coins to fool's gold.'

'There is yet another group burying the fool's gold back into the hill,' added Khalen. 'One of them looks like you, Sneaky.'

'I hear laughing coming from the bank across the stream,' said Sneaky.

'The master is mimicking the laughter of going to the bank,' said Khalen. "It adds to the frustration.

'I think I saw my friend Clumsy McWuzzi. Let's leave this land of trickery,' suggested Sneaky.

'This is nothing but a small sample of this world,' said Khalen. 'We need to see much more of the population. Sneaky, let go your death grip on Petal's hand. I have you securely. Petal will lead us with her light and we will travel more quickly in a straight line.'

Just as Sneaky let go of Petal's hand, a spirit latched onto his dangling arm. It started pulling him, and the other two toward the gold mine.

'Sneaky, do you remember me?' asked the soul in a gravelly voice. 'You tricked me; I never got my pot of gold.'

'Let me go. I don't remember you,' said Sneaky.

'Your luck has run out, you little thief,'

'Grab on,' shouted another soul.

About a hundred other souls latched on and formed a chain connecting all the way to the entrance of the mine.

'Let go of me; I'm not of your world,' pleaded Sneaky.

'Your luck has run out, you little thief,' countered the soul. 'You took my wine and grain, and told me I'd find a pot of gold; I found nothing. I had to steal to pay my debts. You caused me to come here.'

The line jerked them; they fell toward the entrance to the mineshaft. Petal managed to spin; she grabbed Sneaky's hand to break the grasp of the chain of souls. They spun around like a maple seed, and lifted upwards into an orange sky. Wind carried them southerly to what looked like a shadow of Africa. Souls were running from prehistoric elephants and sabre tooth tigers. The beasts won out, but something stranger was happening.

'The hunters have become the hunted,' stated Khalen. 'Poachers are being devoured, regurgitated, and beginning the chase all over again.'

'Why are some of them bound and gagged, and facing the earth?' questioned Sneaky.

'Their punishment is to not see earthly treasures,' said Khalen. 'As for you, my childish leprechaun, you would sit in the corner forever.

*You have been lucky in Hell today. I hope you learned your lesson and
have seen enough to stop testing your luck. I have seen enough.'*

*Sneaky McLittle gave a big sigh of relief, said Count Hugh. As for
me, I wanted them to show me more."*

'This is a horrible way to spend eternity,' stated Petal.

*'To my understanding, there is a review of judgment at each circle,'
explained Khalen. 'To maintain a constant effort from the population,
the Devil offers souls a way to earn their way out of a level. Souls can
move upward and even return to Fairy Knowe. They could even pass
on to the outer universe, depending on the knight guarding the gateway.
Souls have a free will even in punishment. I doubt if any of them have
ever taken the offer.'*

"I was surprised to hear Khalen talk about our mission," said Count
Hugh, breaking from his tale. "He's right about the Devil's offer. Should a
soul ever earn its way out of Hell, the nine of us would convene as a jury
where Hugues would lead the hearing. We could allow the soul to return
to this world only to receive another judgment from God. It is a very rare
occurrence, but let me return to my tale."

'It sounds like false hope to me,' said Petal.

'At least there's some kind of hope,' said Sneaky.

'Let us form a circle for re-entry,' commanded Khalen.

*They re-entered the golden tunnel just as I had some new business,
so to speak. I tossed a new soul into Hell directly at them just as they
were making their ascent. A burst of light and sparkles exploded filling
the tunnel with smoke. They popped out landing before me. The silly
leprechaun rolled his eyes and tugged his beards. He took off as fast as
his feet could carry him. I gave Khalen that look again, my scrunched-
nose look. Jokingly I added, 'I'm glad it's only you; for a moment I
thought the poor soul I just sent to Hell was being rejected. I guess
Sneaky's feeling lucky to be out of there.' He nodded in agreement.*

"That's my tale," said Count Hugh. "Greed does not pay. Did you like
my scrunched face?"

"I liked the tale, your face, and your sense of humor," replied the minister. "You have been an entertaining chap and have told your tale well.
Thank you so much and God be with you."

"Be well, my friend," said the Count of Champagne. "Geoffroi Bison
is waiting his turn. He has a tragic tale of anger and is a bit of a bull him-

self, a bison understands anger." The knight laughed heartily as he floated away from the tree.

"Always keep your sense of humor, my friend!" he shouted back to the minister, "even when a bull is charging at you."

The Count pretended to be a bullfighter as Bison charged towards the tree. Both knights laughed at the encounter.

CHAPTER 8

ANGER MASKS JEALOUSY

eoffroi Bisol at your service, dear minister," announced the next knight.

"The count referred to you as Geoffroi Bison?" questioned the minister.

"That's a nickname he gave me," explained Bisol. "I fought a demon wolf in a battle with our leader Hugues de Payens. The giant wolf had been a terror to farmers in the outlands as well as to citizens on the outskirts of our cities. He fought valiantly and broke three teeth in the battle. When he finally fell, a man appeared in his place and then disappeared into a mist. It was no doubt the Devil's work. My name is Bisol, meaning twin suns. God's will is for me to defend the soul of man in this world and beyond. My anger can be like a bull, but it's controlled."

"I see," said the minister. "I'll pray for you. It's only fitting you stand guard at this gateway. What's your tale of anger about?"

"It's a most tragic tale of anger," explained Bisol. "When anger divides a family it destroys the foundation of mankind's most precious gift, that gift of bonding and belonging to something greater. Family members have a way of connecting; their souls reach out to each other and become stronger as a result. It is tragic when anger breaks down the fabric that binds a family together. Jealousy, pride, and power often lead to arguments that never get resolved. The family bond is precious and sadly many people don't understand how it strengthens or weakens their own soul."

"I agree," said the minister. "I miss my family. One day they will understand the importance of my life. They believe I was placing them in danger with my studies of the fairies, but the danger is real with or without my efforts to protect them. I will resist this fairy king with everything I have. One day, Bisol, we will bask in the light of another sun together. Heaven will be our home and our families will have true joy."

"Your life prepared you for this battle," said Bisol. "Here's my tale."

It was a brisk, windy morning at Circle Five. I was feeling so free that I began singing the children's song Frere Jacques. The fairy queen, Lilliana, rode up the main path of Fairy Knowe on her white stallion looking more as if she was going for a jog in the country than a trip to Hell. She wore a white silk scarf covering much of her silky black hair, the scarf flowing over her shoulders onto her white leather suit. Khalen followed her on his black stallion wearing black leather instead of red; his thick white hair seemed whiter. I had been singing so loudly that I hadn't noticed Olive Flametree and Thorn Cornembers sitting in the garden underneath this tree.

Khalen spotted them and said cheerfully, 'So Thorn, have your embers begun to heat up this morning? Have you noticed any flame in Olive?'

'Do not tease them, my dear,' scolded Lilliana rather mildly. 'I am sure they had a good night's rest for the journey ahead of us.'

'I hope you are right my queen. They look like they have been stoking a fire to me.'

'There is no need to be concerned about me, my king,' said Thorn. 'I could move a mountain today.'

'Good morning King Khalen,' interrupted Olive. 'Thank you for seeing us off.'

'My lady has asked me to join you,' explained Khalen.

'I am still feeling uneasy about the mirage I saw yesterday,' added Lilliana. 'I want the support from my love. My journey to Circle Nine still causes some dizziness as well. My apologies to both of you for breaking our security rule yesterday. We should never have separated.'

'There is no need to apologize,' piped up Thorn, 'I can handle myself and protect Olive from any harm. It brought us closer together. Perhaps one day we will have the kind of closeness you two have.'

'Thorn, say Olive three times,' commanded Khalen not cracking a smile.

'Olive, Olive, Olive...' said Thorn and blushed.

'I know you do,' said Khalen. 'Oh love, I love Olive, the words just roll off your tongue. Oh love, I love Olive my goddess and warrior princess.'

'He is trying to embarrass you, Thorn,' said Olive.

'He has done a good job at that,' said Lilliana. 'Thorn, your hair has spiked even more and your ears are turning red. This is when you need sideburns. I hope you can concentrate on what you need to do.'

'He told me he would grow his sideburns,' added Olive.

'An analysis of this circle leads us to believe we are in for a tiring day,' added Lilliana, a bit irritated with the comment.

'Circle Five contains the souls of the angry,' explained Khalen. 'It is an unstable world filled with confusion. We could never see it all in one trip. There is just too much of it. We have decided to focus on the anger of jealous souls. Today we will be crossing what I refer to as the Ocean of Jealousy.'

'You are probably thinking about lovers,' suggested Lilliana. 'This world contains many forms of jealousy like sister to sister, or grandfather to grandchild. Souls in this ocean draw their anger from a raging river - anything and everything that ever bothered them - and direct it to what makes them jealous. They do not recognize their jealousy; they justify it by things that have hurt their ego. Consumed by anger and in denial of their jealousy they have become clueless to the heart of their problems. You must beware; their anger could get directed at you.'

'Let us join hands. The four of us will enter the gateway on my command,' stated Khalen.

'I feel safe with Thorn,' said Olive.

'Thorn, will you be jealous if Olive holds my hand?' asked Khalen.

'Not at all, you are the King,' said Thorn.

'Keep that in mind throughout the journey,' said Khalen.

They formed their circle and spun into the gateway at Khalen's command. When they entered, I was surprised to follow their every move. Never before had I seen the inside of the tunnel. It was metallic gray; spinning chains powered by a rough wind enveloped each fairy causing them to break their grip. Squeezed tighter and tighter by the ordeal, they looked to be in pain. Suddenly, out of nowhere, an angry soul came at me hard, no doubt needing to get to her destination. Yes, she was an angry, impulsive woman, rude to her own detriment.

'Get out of my way,' she demanded.

"I gave her what she asked for. Another soul followed her calling her Pocha, but she did not seem to care about him. I flicked him easily into Hell and looked to see what happened.

To my amazement, chubby Pocha flew past the fairies causing them to break away from their chains. Olive grabbed Thorn by his foot and Thorn latched on to Khalen's ankle while Lilliana and Khalen joined hands. With Khalen and Lilliana in the lead, they emerged into a reddish-yellow sky over a slimy green ocean, an ocean thick and tangled. Pocha splashed down hard and moments later the fellow following her splashed down.

The fairies drifted in space above the two condemned souls. Ahead of them, sparkles illuminated from shifting, sinking black sand on a coastline. The sand looked dangerous as if it were a black hole swallowing everything, even time. A raging river, red as bad blood and seemingly angry at the ocean, broke the coastline. Pocha and her follower headed towards the river near the coast.

A tail wind began to grow stronger; it forced the fairies lower and lower, to descend just above the two souls heading towards the mouth of the river.

Khalen shouted, 'We must be strong with this wind; there is no place to land. I have studied this area from above. The two souls are fighting river currents against ocean tide. I want to speak to the woman.'

'They must be exhausted,' said Olive.

Managing the wind, Khalen took them to a few feet over the ocean, above Pocha now entering the mouth of the river.

'You must be exhausted,' called Olive. 'There is a piece of driftwood under the water to your right. It will help you save your energy.'

'You're very nosey,' shouted Pocha. 'When I want your opinion, I'll ask for it. Do you think you're smarter than me?'

'She was only trying to help you,' said Thorn. 'Why are you so angry?'

'It's none of your business,' shouted the woman. 'No one has suffered more than me. I don't need your insults. Insults after insults are all I ever got, even from my sister.'

'How did she insult you?' questioned Khalen.

'She told me I was overweight and rude,' replied the woman.

'Look at you,' stated Khalen. 'You are overweight and rude. Perhaps you should have listened to her.'

'Did you ever talk to her like sisters do?' asked Olive.

'You're a real jerk,' said the woman. 'Anyway, she's dead to me; she's dead to the family.'

'You are the one who is dead,' stated Khalen. 'Let me guess. Your sister was thin and beautiful and lived the life you dreamed of."

'Go to Hell,' said Pocha, 'You're a pain in my ass!'

'As far as I can tell,' said Khalen, 'you are in Hell, at the mouth of the bloody River of Anger having come from the green envy Ocean of Jealousy. You did not get here for trying to resolve things with your sister.'

'Find your inner peace,' interjected Lilliana.

'What do you want?' demanded the woman.

'We only wanted to help,' replied Lilliana.

'Leave me alone,' insisted Pocha, 'I don't want to talk to any of you ever again.'

'Why do you not wait for the fellow following you?' questioned Thorn.

'He's an idiot,' was all she said.

The fairies watched her as she entered the River of Anger, complaining and cursing, and blaming everything that went wrong in her life on someone else. She struggled to swim to shore and crawled on to the black sand; moments later the Sands of Time swallowed her. The fairies began their ascent to leave. Looking back, they saw Pocha emerge in the ocean, only to start her journey again. The faint sound of groans on a swirling wind followed the fairies out of Circle Five to the tunnel of chains. Slowly they fought the winds and the chains until they collapsed in exhaustion at my feet.

Again, I sang Frere Jacques; they ignored me.

"That's my sad tale," said the knight. "A sister should never give up trying to be a sister. It defies the laws of the universe. God bless you minister. I must return to my post."

"Keep singing my good bull, Bisol," said Kirk. "I will pray for your family after I pray for mine."

"I will pray for your family too. You are a remarkable soul, Minister Kirk. Despite the fairies best efforts to steal your soul, you still pray for others. What keeps you strong?"

"Memories with my family keep me going, something as simple as having lamb shank with potatoes and fresh bread with my wife and children. I see their rosy cheeks and smiling faces in the candlelight. Standing in the doorway of my small church and thanking God for the gift of life keeps me strong. Vivid memories with my sister in my childhood are so precious. It troubles me to hear stories like yours; evil comes in different forms. Without my family, life would mean very little."

"I understand," said the knight. "Counting you, there are now ten of us guarding the gates of Hell; we are a brotherhood. We think of you in those terms. Until we meet our own families again, we are your family. Your next visitor is quite different than most of us. He is Rossal, one of our two monks."

Kirk expected another visitor to come right away, but that was not possible. Khalen inflicted another barrage of red waves traversing within the cells of the tree; it lasted for days if not weeks. Time was unrecognizable.

Khalen decided to clamp down on his prized possession, having witnessed the knights travelling back and forth to the tree. Although, he had no real concern for the knights and their curiosity, he felt the need to assert his power.

CHAPTER 9

Communicating Through Dreams

Red wave after red wave bombarded Minister Kirk. A pattern emerged and the beleaguered soul discovered a way to detect waves in advance. By withdrawing into a deep shell of meditation, he avoided negative thoughts before they could set in. He had no concept of time only that the attacks became longer and longer. A spark of light started the wave; a sense of coolness occurred when it ended. At last, Khalen gave his power source a rest.

It seemed like ages since Bisol had visited him. Finally, a surprise visitor took the opportunity to check in on the embattled minister; it was the grand master, Hugues de Payens.

"You've had quite an ordeal, dear minister," said Hugues. "We've been praying for you. How are you?"

"I feel your prayers, and I'm the same as ever, happy to hear about those demon fairies in Hell."

"I'm sorry to interrupt your tales; but I have some bad news for you. It's concerning your son, Robert E. Kirk Jr."

"Have the fairies harmed him?" asked the minister. "He's just a child."

"Not yet," said Hugues. "He's an adult now and ready to begin his ministry. The fairy folk are concerned about him following your passion and preaching your same message. You discovered the secret to entering this world; that made you a major threat. Fairies are convinced your son will follow your lead. The argument between Khalen's *Tolerants* and his adversaries, the *Raptorials* with their allies, the *Dissidents*, has intensified. *Raptorials* and *Dissidents* have increased their abductions and terror. Khalen wants them to stop. He's pleading for more time and reassuring them that he's close to taking possession of your soul. King Odin, one of the three other leaders, wants to eliminate your son. Khalen wants to use him. You will want to join us in prayer for your son."

"Oh, my God," said the minister. "I will do what I can. How long have I been here?"

"Time is different in this world; five decades back home have passed," explained Hugues. "Pray for him."

"He has no gift of second sight. Becoming a pastor at my church would be dangerous for him," said Kirk. "He must serve somewhere else. Our family needs him for protection."

"I understand," said the knight. "He is your kindred and therefore a threat. His fate is inevitable; one day he will join the fight for your soul and the soul of man."

"Fight for my soul?" questioned the minister.

"The war over you has taken on a new dimension. In addition to the conflict with the fairies, all souls, good and bad, have united to fight for your soul. They do this by harassing fairies whenever they can. It's actually making our jobs as knights more difficult. Evil souls are taking advantage of the crises."

"What could happen to my son?" asked the minister.

"It is inevitable that one day your son will die; he will pass through to this realm and discover your fate."

"I see," said the minister.

"He will need to decide whether to fight for you or move on to his destiny. God will support his decision."

"That's encouraging, but what can a lifeless body do?" questioned Kirk.

"Although we have no physical presence, you above all others know the fear we bring to the fairy. They don't understand the soul and they're fearful of us. All souls recognize this fear and terrorize fairies whenever possible. Unless Khalen is successful and takes control over souls, your son will join the fight. Every day Khalen works hard to master his skills over the human mind."

"I have felt his power. He is constantly trying to influence my thoughts. Lilith began the battle as soon as God replaced her with Eve. They were the Watchers for Noah. In the desert for forty days, they tried to tempt Jesus into giving them a soul. Their attacks are relentless."

"I have witnessed Khalen's ability to influence fear and temptation in weak souls," explained the knight. "He has absolute control over captured humans in this world. They are completely dependent on him and even love him and their leaders. His power is strengthening now that he has captured you."

"I am fighting his attacks by keeping my focus on other things. I wish I could do more."

"There's nothing you can do, except pray," said the grand master. "We will keep you informed and do what we can. It is best that you continue learning about this world and Hell. Here comes Rossal now. He was a world-class monk before becoming a knight, one very capable of handling his circle."

"Thank you," called Rossal, suddenly joining them. "I heard you mentioning prayer. It is my specialty. Fair folk have no concept about its energy and power. How could they? They study us and find the process fascinating. I am praying for you Minister Kirk and your son every chance I get."

"God bless you and thank you," said the minister.

"I only wish we still had the Holy Nail," stated Rossal. "It was a wonderful relic and weapon through the crusades."

"Tell me about it," said the minister. "I can see it is a source of pride for all of you."

"The story is better told by Godfrey de Saint-Omer," said Rossal.

"That's true," said Hugues. "I'm sure you remember him. He told you the first tale. The Holy Nail came from the right hand of Jesus at the cross. Godfrey and I received it in Jerusalem from a citizen. He gave it to us to protect the relic for fear of losing it during the war. We forged the nail into a ring and I wore it around my neck on a gold chain. It was a major source of inspiration for us; many pilgrims understand its power."

"It harnesses the great power of prayer," added Rossal.

"That it does; I must return to my post now," said Hugues. "I will ask the others to pray with us. Godfrey will tell you the tale properly." He drifted from the tree towards his post at the Devil's doorstep.

"Before I begin," said Rossal, "I have to tell you what happened before the fairies went through the gateway. The woodlands creatures around Circle Six were unusually restless one morning not too long ago. On the other hand, was it a long time ago? I'm not sure. I was very busy praying for two souls that I was holding by the scruff of their necks. Before tossing them into Hell, I heard two fairies arguing about their turtles. They were so loud and passionate about who had won a race. I stopped to listen; suddenly, one of the souls I was holding shriveled up and was sucked into Hell before I gave him a toss. A very bad one he was; but this is where my tale begins."

"I'm sorry to stop you," said the minister. "I'm sure your tale is fine, but I'd rather you help me pray for my son right now. I can't stop worrying about him."

"I understand," said Rossal. "Whenever I'm worried about a loved one, which is quite often, I meditate to a white light in my mind's eye to pray for the person. "Have you ever done that?"

"Are you talking about moonlight or starlight?" asked the minister.

"In meditation, the white light is in my mind," explained Rossal. "It starts off like a flicker and grows in strength. I focus on the person and use the light like a healing tool. Perhaps you should try that with your son. You have a wonderful bond. I'm certain you could reach him in his dreams."

"I will try that," said Kirk. "Instead of telling me your tale today, can you help me with this?"

"Most certainly," said Rossal, "this is what monks do best."

The two of them prayed continuously; the minister was very impressed with the monk's stamina. They concentrated on Robert E. Kirk Jr. and the white light. Deep into their meditation, Hugues de Payens interrupted them.

"Rossal, my dear friend," said the grandmaster. "You must return to your post; I can no longer cover your circle as well as mine. I know you've been praying instead of storytelling."

"Your prayers achieved results. Today, at the breakfast table of Robert E. Kirk Jr., the young minister stated that he had a dream about his father. Reverend Kirk, you appeared before your son; you were in your church and gave your blessing for your son to take a ministry position in another church. He said that you told him to take up the battle for man's soul in his own way and not make the mistake you made. The family was relieved and thrilled with his decision. They agreed to have no further mention of fairies. Your praying was successful; you reached him in his dreams."

"Thank God," said the minister.

"You have special skills," said Rossal. "You made a connection with your son without your soul travelling. That was truly remarkable."

"I reached my cousin Graham once when he was dreaming, but that was the day I died. You helped me with this and I am so grateful. I could have never reached him without you."

"We are a brotherhood," said Rossal.

"We must return to our posts," interjected Hugues. "Godfrey will return to tell you the story of the Holy Nail. He won't be able to wait until the others tell their tales. I'm sure you won't mind a break from Hell."

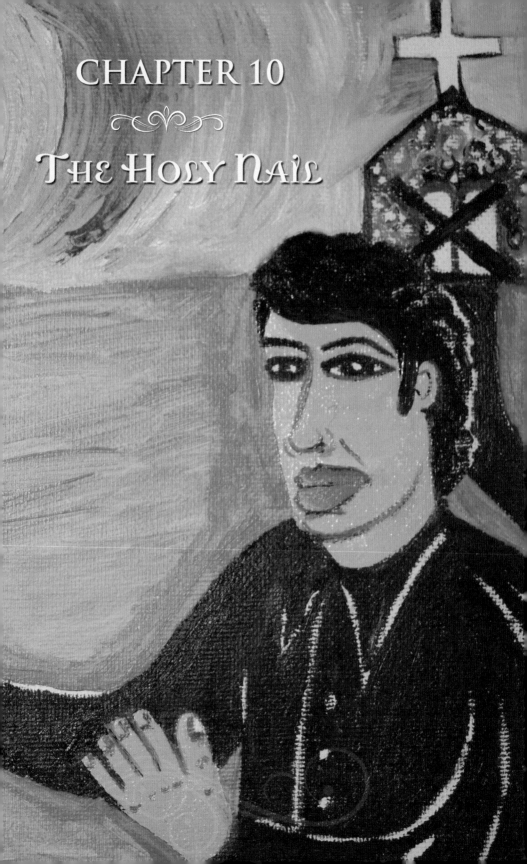

CHAPTER 10

THE HOLY NAIL

odfrey de Saint Omer gladly left his position at Circle One to be with Reverend Kirk. The story of the Holy Nail was his favorite; he never tired of telling it.

"Hello, Minister Kirk," said the cheerful knight. "I understand you're taking a break from hearing about the parallel worlds of Hell and want to hear a good story."

"I'm very concerned about my son," said the minister. "These fairy folk are dangerous. I understand the Holy Nail has power; perhaps it could be a weapon to protect my son. I want to learn all about it."

"The Holy Nail was a great weapon during the crusades," explained Godfrey. "Its last whereabouts was with relatives of Payne de Monteverdi, the knight at Circle Two. Getting it to your son would take a minor miracle. I would never dismiss it as a possibility. There are no boundaries when it comes to depth of thought from our Savior. Perhaps he knew the iron nail in his right hand would be a weapon in the battle for the soul. I can only say for certain Hugues and I felt its power immediately when we were given the relic."

"You give me great hope, Sir Godfrey.

On August 1 in the year 1100, began the knight, Hugues and I were nearing the end of a hot, dusty journey to Jerusalem, riding on a single horse. We could afford only one beast on this return trip, having been there the year before. It was our mission to fight religious persecution.

Many Christians were happy to see our return; we could see their smiles and hope returning to their faces. Most seemed afraid to approach us when suddenly a brave yet humble fellow rushed to greet us in the street. He told us his name was Titus and thanked us for coming to them for they all had been praying for our return. He offered us lodging and a place to care for our horse. He wanted to give us food and water, apologizing for not having any wine. We accepted his invitation, of course.

Titus dropped to his knees and thanked God for sending us. In his brief prayer, he mentioned the fear he had for his family for he was in possession of a very sacred item.

As soon as he said 'Amen,' he stood up, and without hesitation, he came forth with the sacred relic. It was an iron nail, but not a simple nail for it was very smooth and polished. He explained it was one of the iron nails from Christ's crucifixion, and that this nail had come from *the right hand of the Savior. The four-inch iron nail was very smooth and polished, just like other artifacts handled extensively during prayer services. This Holy Nail had been the object of worship for eleven centuries. Hugues said a prayer and we took turns kissing the relic.*

Titus no longer wanted the responsibility for the Holy Nail. He was afraid for his life and the possibility of the sacred artifact ending up in the hands of the enemy. He demanded that we take it.

We accepted the holy relic without hesitation. I insisted that Hugues have the honor of carrying it. He held the nail close to his heart. The emotion he felt was so strong; he said that he would carry it close to his heart at all times.

Transporting it became a great concern; we did not want to take any risk of losing it. I made a suggestion about putting the nail on a chain. That seemed like a good idea but still too risky. Hugues suggested we form the nail into a ring and attach it to a chain. We agreed to change the shape of the nail to make it more secure in travel. After much debate about changing the shape of the relic, we took the Holy Nail to a God-fearing blacksmith.

The local blacksmith, a holy man, forged the iron nail into a ring by curving and tucking the point of the nail underneath its flat head to form a circle. The head of the nail sat like a jewel on a band. The clever blacksmith engraved a figure on the head of the nail. He made a wavy line, representing the back of our horse, and two crosses representing the two of us carrying the cross of Christ. The blacksmith removed a gold chain from around his neck. He put the ring on the chain and handed it to me.

I kissed the relic and thanked him. I then looked at Hugues and said, 'Hugues, you will lead the crusades and change the world. I pledge my support to you. Coming from the right hand of Christ, to be worn over your heart, I present to you the Holy Nail.'

Upon placing the chain around my good friend's neck, the Christian sighed, the blacksmith wept, and I shed tears. Hugues comforted us, stating that all men should have the same opportunity as him to know the meaning of love from wearing this sacred relic.

Hugues told the blacksmith that God would reward him. To the Christian, Titus, he promised protection for his family and the Holy Nail.

That was the real beginning of the Knights Templar. Hugues became the grand master; together we enlisted seven other knights from

France and England to make nine in total. You have met many of them. The small engraving on the Holy Nail later became our seal; it represents our humble beginning. I am proud to say that we nine knights created a legacy to protect the souls of men from persecution; our work continues at the nine gateways to Hell.

Just as Godfrey de Saint Omer concluded his tale, Hugues returned with more unsettling news.

"Godfrey, my friend," said his leader, "there is much unrest on the hill. As you know, all souls are in an uproar about the minister's incarceration. Evil ones taking up the fight have made our jobs more difficult. We have much work to do to get the evil ones where they belong."

"I've just completed my tale," said Godfrey. "Minister Kirk would like us to find a way to somehow get the Holy Nail to his son. We need to pray on this matter. Perhaps we can allow some ghosts to make life unbearable for Khalen. A bit of a delay in sending the buggers to Hell would not be all bad."

"Don't let my situation put you at risk for losing an evil soul," cautioned the minister.

"I like the idea of finding the Holy Nail," stated Hugues. "This is a matter of priorities. We will find a way."

"Would fairies retaliate against my family and my congregation for ghosts defending me?" questioned the minister.

"Fairies can be very vengeful and nasty," stated Hugues. "They fight each other, but rarely has anyone ever been hurt."

"My concern is there may be more baby abductions," stated the minister.

"Khalen has some control on this issue," said Godfrey. "He's called for a halt on this practice to gain time in seducing the soul; he will fight to get his way. The others risk a great deal in challenging him; Khalen controls the human population in this world. He has the power to make life very uncomfortable for everyone. The conflict is brewing though. His adversaries are terrified about an invasion as a result of your book."

"I gather he controls his abductees with the red energy?" questioned Kirk.

"That's true," said Hugues. "He uses it on you constantly."

"He told me about it when he captured me," said Kirk. "This is a powerful weapon."

"Pray, good minister, for the Holy Nail," said Hugues. "We will join you for prayers often get results through dreams. You have become the battle line for man's soul. We must return to our posts now."

"Thank you for everything, especially your story about the Holy Nail," said Kirk. "God has prepared me for this battle. I will show Him I'm worthy."

Later that same day Minister Kirk looked through the portal to his church across from Doon Hill. He was elated to see his son Robert E. Kirk Jr. with his daughter Marjorie, and his son's second wife, Lilias, approach his church, once again boarded up. They could not enter so they walked to the mock grave. Kirk Jr. kneeled by the grave; Lilias and Marjorie also bowed their heads to pray.

From the main path of Doon Hill came a knight on horseback racing across the field towards Kirk Jr. and his family. He rode swiftly, unnoticed by the family in deep prayer. As the rider got closer to them, Kirk Jr. looked up. Startled at the Knight's intensity, Kirk directed his wife and sister to run; they headed toward the boarded-up church.

The Knight galloped up to Kirk Jr. at the grave, "Fear not a member of the Knights Templar. I have a gift for your family. I am George Payne; my ancestor was one of the original knights. I've been riding for two days to reach you after having a vivid dream involving my ancestor and your father."

Kirk Jr. called out to his family to remain calm and that he was in no danger. The knight dismounted. He wore a white robe with a red cross and removed the hood from over his head. Looking back to Doon Hill, he saluted Minister Kirk.

"While I am a skeptical man, I have no misgivings about the treasure I'm about to give you. You must understand clearly, that this matter carries great significance for the future of all men. Do not take this encounter lightly."

The knight held out his left hand and opened it to reveal the Holy Nail in the form of a ring on a gold chain.

"Your father is in great danger of losing his soul. This will affect all men. Your family needs this relic to protect your souls. This is one of the Holy Nails from Christ's crucifixion. Forged into a ring centuries ago, it was the main source of inspiration for the Knights Templar including an ancestor of mine, Payne de Monteverdi. Hold it close to your heart when you pray. We do not give you this gift lightly. It is very much needed in the battle with fairies."

"Thank you for your concern," said Marjorie, returning to her brother along with Lilias. "Upon my mother's last breath she ordered that we no longer speak of fairy folk. What you have here will bring us misery."

"My sister speaks the truth," agreed Kirk Jr. "My father's wishes were that I pursue a different ministry than his. I will not take up his cause."

"Take the ring," said the knight placing the relic in Kirk's hand with a handshake, "It provides protection for us all."

The knight pulled his hood over his head and returned to his horse. "Heed my words for I am a freemason. The battle for the soul of man is in every heart."

He mounted his horse and galloped back across the field towards Doon Hill.

"It does not look like a nail," said Lilias.

"Who are the freemasons, anyway?" questioned Marjorie. "Are they pretending to be knights from the crusades?"

"I think he means well," said Kirk Jr. "It looks like a relic. We shall put it in a safe place. Our ancestors will appreciate the story even if it's not true."

"Imagine the likelihood of us receiving an actual nail from the cross of our Savior," said Lilias.

"The townspeople will shun and mock us even more should they find out about this," added Marjorie.

"In no way can my father's book ever be published," said Kirk Jr. "There would be much retribution from the fairies. Should this ring be authentic, it could not stop that. We will speak nothing about this encounter. Let's finish our prayer and never return to this site again."

From high atop the massive pine tree, Minister Kirk observed the scenario. He prayed, "Please God, help my family to understand the gift they've been given. Help them to understand the power of the Holy Nail."

CHAPTER 11

UNREST

minister Kirk was in deep meditation, nearly oblivious to the world around him, when the voices of Lilliana and Khalen broke his concentration.

"Khalen, my love," said Lilliana, "you have been working nonstop. My crimson roses have been in full bloom and you have missed their peak. I have missed your company."

"I am close to a major breakthrough, my beautiful lady," said Khalen. "Come my dear; look at what I have installed in the garden. It is a control box harnessing earth's power; these probes connect to the cellular structure of the tree and can send more of everything to the minister. Light waves, sound waves, and even fragrances penetrate the tree. A constant stream of data is giving me valuable information about fear and temptation in the human mind."

"I do not think I could ever understand this," said Lilliana. "Is not the minister deceased? How can he have a mind?"

"I do not understand it either," admitted Khalen. "I only know that the soul, his spirit, continues to function and grow. Think of the soul as a seed. A small pine seed carries everything it needs to grow tall. Some seeds are stronger, just like this tree that stands taller than any tree on the hill. The minister's soul carries everything he needs for eternity. I am gathering that information to compare it to our own cellular structure."

"Some of the lights are starting to quiver," said Lilliana. Does the minister feel them?"

From deep within the tree, the minister experienced a deep red light, a low pulsation, and a flowery fragrance.

"My experiment is yielding some adjustments in his soul, defense mechanisms. Given the results, I believe he must feel the combination I have put together. Currently I am studying loneliness."

"I am a bit uncomfortable with all this," said Lilliana. "You look so handsome in your red suit. Please put this aside and talk with me. I received some information about protesters in Falias again today."

"What are they complaining about?"

"They are claiming a group of humans carrying iron weapons are very close to a gateway near Gorias, and demanding to know what you are doing with the minister. They obviously do not like your handling of this matter, claiming that King Odin will launch an attack to protect his city with or without your support."

"These claims are false reports. Odin wants to be the first to get a soul," said Khalen. "He would not do anything rash to lose that possibility. He also knows I could create an unhappy workforce for him. The story has been made up to put pressure on me."

"Pressure is coming from everywhere. Ghosts of every kind throughout our world are committing acts of terror," explained Lilliana. "Protesters are claiming they are organizing an attack to be made from the living."

"I know firsthand that Kirk's folk want no part of us. They have prevented the printing of the minister's book to avoid any problems from us. They do not intend to follow their minister. Should anything change concerning their fear of us, then I will handle it. Any attack from our side could provoke more ministers to search for us. We need to wait and see what becomes of Kirk's book and discoveries. We must change how we deal with them. Human folk are growing in intelligence, but still primitive in handling their emotions."

"We live in a fragile world," said Lilliana. "None of the other leaders support you. Brighid, with her pet dragons, and Odin with his ravens and wolves would never accept your analysis. Everything they believe about human folk tells them to keep humans afraid of us. Brighid lounges in her oasis and does nothing but complain. Odin sits atop one of his mountains and sends nothing but messages of fear on the wind. Lady Vivienne could be of help, but she does a lot of business by sea with both of them. They do not appreciate you; they do not respect that it is your intelligence allowing them to prosper."

"I have provided them with so much," said Khalen, "but they want more. Productive workers under my control have made their lives so easy. Odin relaxes on a mountain and watches his happy workers in the fields.

Brighid would struggle in the desert were it not for the workers bringing in everything she needs. They work at night while she sleeps under the comfort of her blue dome. Where would Vivienne's shipping business be without the laborers doing the tough jobs at sea? They have become very comfortable because of me."

"You are the only one who could give them a soul," added Lilliana.

"No one could do more with the minister's soul. I am the only one with the technology to handle its twenty-one grams of mass powered by six-tenths of a volt of electricity. I will break down the gene at the center of its being."

"You are a true genius and a great leader, my love. No one else follows our code better than you do. The others do not really seem to understand how love can conquer all. None of them could have captured the minister's soul."

"He should not have trespassed into our world."

"How will we deal with the constant panic about a human invasion? These false claims produce great anxiety amongst the steadfast of our supporters. *Raptorials* love to push buttons. They agitate *Dissidents*, especially nasty witches and banshees, to create chaos. How can we stop ghosts from terrorizing everyone?"

"I will find a way to diffuse this situation. Much of it comes from jealousy of you, my queen. They are jealous of your grace and beauty. I may need to exert my power and remind them as to who holds the key to their eternity. Forgive me dear," said Khalen gently, "I must return to my experiment. Have our musicians and dancers practice a routine for you. I will join you for some entertainment. I hear your stallion racing up the hill. Do not worry about silly protests. Time is on our side."

Honey Driftsfur suddenly came galloping up the path on Lilliana's white stallion. She had a human baby in her arms. Khalen and Lilliana rushed to her. Honey handed the small child to Lilliana. It was a beautiful little girl wearing a knitted sweater with the initials "M.O." The child puckered her lower lip but did not cry. Khalen assisted Honey in dismounting the stallion.

"What have we here?" asked Lilliana.

"I saved her life," said Honey. "The witch Baba Yaga was about to boil her alive. A large crowd gathered near the Meteoric Rock after the hag landed in her tree hut. Regina Spideroaster was with her. I thought Regina had learned a lesson from her visit to Hell, but she was there. The hag held this child above a pot in defiance of your orders King Khalen.

She stated she was not only continuing abductions, but that she would eat this child. I confronted her and snatched the child from her."

"What happened then?" asked Khalen.

"As I was riding away, I saw witches heading toward the Museum of Flowers," said Honey. "I stopped long enough to see them talking to Olive Flametree and Sneaky McLittle. *Raptorials* cannot be trusted even after you have shown them Hell."

"This practice must come to an end," said Khalen.

"What will you do with the child?" asked Lilliana.

"I will send her to my cousin, Moth Beamfrost, in Gorias," said Honey. "She is actually a fortunate child. She will receive far better care in our world. The mountain air will be good for her. Occasionally she can return to Fairy Knowe to visit us."

The abduction that day was only the tip of the iceberg for Khalen. After Honey Driftsfur made her report, two other guards, Beetle Willowleaf and Thorn Cornembers continued with what happened after Honey rode away with the baby. Minister Kirk listened carefully to all the reports.

Beetle Willowleaf began, "As Honey Driftsfur was riding away, Baba Yaga had a temper tantrum. The witch caused the pot of boiling oil to explode. Her hut lifted off the ground making a small tornado sending everyone into hysteria."

"The crowd rushed to the Museum of Flowers," added Cornembers. "Other witches, including Regina Spideroaster, flew wildly around the building. Banshees stood at the entrance moaning and wailing while the rest of the despicable dregs ransacked the museum, stealing precious artifacts. Crystal black roses were stolen."

"Precious amaranth preserved since the time of the Great Infiltration of Incas was taken among other things," continued Willowleaf. "A fossil of the world's first flowering plant from one-hundred and twenty-five million years ago (found off the coast of China) was shattered. We collected the small pieces and placed them in a wooden box."

"We spotted the leprechaun, Sneaky McLittle with the woodlander Chestnut Silvertwist paying looters," added Cornembers. "It is hard to understand how they have become involved fresh off their missions to Hell."

"I have not shared this part with Thorn yet," stated Willowleaf, "I am sorry Thorn. Silvertwist somehow convinced Olive Flametree to join him; Chestnut and Olive were seen shaking hands with Sneaky after he had paid the last looter."

"Are you certain about Olive?" questioned Thorn.

"I am certain; as they were shaking hands, a terrible storm arose," continued Willowleaf. "Thunder cracked and lightning struck the Meteoric Rock. *Dissidents* fled the city with the storm at their back. I cannot help but think that Odin was aiding in their escape. We were paralyzed by the wind and lightning, helpless to arrest the protesters."

"We have much work to do," said Khalen.

Another guard, Petal Hailfrost, came running into the garden, "I have more reports of incidents," she announced. "Bad weather conditions aided several demonstrations near the city of Gorias. Dregs from the region protested an end-of-the-world scenario with a false report of a planned human invasion. It is suspected that King Odin provided a torrential downpour for the Dissidents to add to the effect and there is more." She gave the report to Lilliana.

"In the southern region of Finias," read the queen, "Brighid allowed her dragons to participate in a demonstration with hobgoblins; they created a massive fire portraying the end of the world."

"In Murias," she continued, "Lady Vivienne banned all ocean vessels to come in our direction to Falias. She claims that we have put her city in danger of a tsunami. Our city is off limits. We are considered to be an unsafe destination, and at high risk for a human invasion."

"Here is a report from Gwynn ap Nuud's Underworld," added Petal. "Massive amounts of bugs, snakes, and spiders have been migrating to Falias. Even a resurgence of the four-hundred-million-year-old Devonian rhyniognatha has been spotted along with other prehistoric insects. Falias is doomed. I suspect that King Gwynn ap Nuud, is rallying the insect world. He has joined forces with the other three leaders."

"Oh my," said Lilliana, "tent cities are popping up everywhere; witches, hags, hobgoblins, and all the dregs of society are gathering for a Doomsday Celebration ahead of the big invasion."

"None of these leaders understand my power," said Khalen. "Odin has mastered weather. Brighid has harnessed the sun's energy, and Vivienne has mastered sea power; but I have the power of the earth, a combination of all their powers. I can influence the mind of our enemy, something they could never do. Their only hope at achieving eternal life is through me. They are fools to challenge me."

"They are afraid, my King," said Lilliana. "Let us mourn our losses for now."

The loss of artifacts from the Museum of Flowers was very depressing. Lilliana decorated the garden underneath the minister's pine tree with black roses and replicas of the small ancient flowering water plant. Two musicians, a harpist and a cellist, played mournful songs while Lilliana directed the crew with their decorations.

A small table, situated directly underneath the tree, was in direct line of sight for the minister to see and hear their conversation. He could see the small wooden box carrying the shattered fossil plant in the center of the table with a crystal black rose at its side.

"While we disagree on some things, I never expected this kind of reaction from Raptorials," said Khalen. "Capturing the minister's soul has caused me more grief than ever."

"They are frightened because the minister was walking into the portal when he had his heart attack," said Lilliana. "He discovered how to enter our world and could have been a huge danger. It was fortunate for us that he died in the process."

"Your point is well taken, my love," said Khalen. "I must speed up my efforts to transfer his soul. These demonstrations are getting out of hand. Before us lies one of earth's most precious fossils in total ruin. The black rose has given me an idea."

"Tell me, my love."

"I am going to transmit a darker, deeper red burst of energy into the tree," explained Khalen. "If these demonstrations continue, I will send a clear demonstration of power to my adversaries. Through the four granite towers and the Meteoric Rock in Falias I will transmit my new red waves to disrupt the harmony in each city and the Underworld. I will send them a clear and convincing response to their rebelliousness."

"That sounds dangerous," said Lilliana.

"There is no danger to our folk. The energy has a very positive effect on us," explained Khalen. "The energy bursts will have major effects on human folk. Brighid, Odin, and Lady Vivienne will have to deal with their human population. There could be anything from mass hysteria to mass depression. They will respect me and beg me to maintain peace and harmony."

"I hope it does not come to that," said Lilliana. "Lady Vivienne has just rebuilt Murias after a devastating tidal wave. Odin has made huge improvements to Gorias after the tornado ripped between the two mountains. The blue dome that protects Finias is so fragile; I can't imagine what it must be like to live in the desert."

"Hopefully, I will have a breakthrough this evening with the minister and all this speculation will be for naught."

"Shall we bury the plant now?" asked Lilliana with tears welling up in her deep blue eyes.

"We shall give this the respect it deserves and then I must get to work," replied Khalen.

They dug a small hole at the edge of the garden and buried the remains of the oldest flowering plant on earth. Tears were in their eyes; Khalen placed the crystal black rose within a box. He made a promise to himself to avenge the crime.

As soon as Khalen escorted Lilliana back to the palace, he went to his war room. He transmitted a low pulse of energy that changed the color of the cells within the tree to a deep black red. The pulse would gradually increase with intensity through the night. He left his war room in a hurry to mount his black stallion. The night had no moon, but the darkness did not slow down the stallion. They raced to Falias and proceeded to the red granite tower. This was where Khalen had complete control of the energy surging through the meteorite. To his delight, the lightning strikes earlier in the day had left the rock in a heightened state.

Its great source of power had been previously untapped by the good folk. To this point, the rock had only been a source of inspirational energy. Khalen connected the rock to each of his granite towers. Megaliths are natural conductors, and from the blue granite tower he sent an equal surge of energy to the monolith in the heart of Murias in the west. From the beige granite tower he sent and equal surge of energy directly to the great blue dome that protected the oasis city in the south, Finias. Gorias, with its gold-capped ancient building at its center, received energy directly from the gold granite tower. Khalen sent another surge to that city in the east. The Underworld received surges throughout the earth from the base of the red tower.

Along with the surge, Khalen also sent this message: "I have the human soul, and I will handle the human situation. I will not tolerate lawlessness. This little demonstration of power is but a sample of my new-found strength. Any further protests on your part will be dealt with in a harsh manner."

The electromagnetic surge was so powerful; every flower in each city caught fire instantaneously. Massive changes in emotions from anger to depression gripped the human population; confusion and terror struck the fairy world.

Khalen returned to Fairy Knowe just before dawn. The moon was rising and the sun was not far behind it. He went directly to his war room where he checked his monitors on Minister Kirk. There were no results. The minister had gone into a shell.

Khalen rushed to the circle garden and shouted, "You are no longer a minister of your species; you are my minister. Your soul will be mine. I have given all your folk in my world a taste of my red wave, what you are receiving every day. This is just a beginning of what is in store for your people. You can end this nightmare now. Surrender your soul to me."

CHAPTER 12

WAR BEGINS

Rossal, the monk turned knight, finally paid another visit to the minister, "We know you've had a very dark spell. Many days have passed since the attack on you by the black crystal rose. I've been here many times, always praying for you. How is your spirit?"

"Welcome, dear friend," said Minister Kirk. "I am the same. Have you brought me any news about my son or have you come to tell your tale of Hell?"

"I can report that your son received the Holy Nail. Unfortunately, he and the family made a decision to tuck it away in fear of public opinion. Equally sad, is that your son is nearing the end of his days on earth. I continue to pray for him to have a long life. He could accomplish much should he reconsider his position about the Holy Nail."

He paused for a moment, but there was no response from the minister.

The knight continued, "This also would not be a good time for him to pass into this world. In defense of your incarceration, all souls, regardless of whether they are good, bad, or indifferent, have waged war against the fairies to have you released. To complicate things, fairies are at war with each other. This is not a war with bloodshed, but still a war nonetheless. I pray your son lives a long life. It would not be good for him to pass into all this hysteria. Shall I entertain you with my tale of Circle Six?"

"What's this news about a war between the fairies?" asked the minister.

"I'm sorry; of course, you would be unaware of the attack on Falias," said Rossal.

"I remember that Khalen and Lilliana were very upset about the demonstration at the Museum of Flowers. He was about to send a strong power surge. What has happened?"

"My tale from Hell, I pray, can wait until another day," said the knight. "I happened to be in Falias that day chasing down a heretic. The war began with the surge. This magnificent ancient city, surrounded by granite walls and adorned with gemstones, is now uninhabited and under siege. High in the red tower, Khalen controls power surges emanating from the Meteoric Rock. He transmits energy through all the granite towers. To combat this, enemy dragons rain down fire and smoke on this embattled city every day, but I'm getting ahead of the story."

"Be calm," said the minister, "you can tell me your tale of Hell another time. Please tell me as much as you can about this war."

The knight said a little prayer and began his recollection of how it began. "It was a gray, stormy kind of day, typical of the season when thousands, if not a million butterfly-like messengers descended on Falias. Some were very small, yet others were as large as pumpkins; they were all colorful wind knots and sylphs, no doubt sent by King Odin from Gorias. These beautiful spirits brought a single message to the inhabitants of the city: *Pressure King Khalen to take decisive action to prevent an invasion by humans from the other world.*"

Rossal paused to say a prayer and continued, "Banshees assembled outside the city gates; they started wailing about doomsday. An army of witches, goblins, hags, trolls and others passed them by to follow the butterfly-like messengers. They assembled at the meteorite at the heart of the city. The wind knots and sylphs were so numerous that they covered the black meteorite with a bright collage of colors. The crowd around the massive rock stood in total silence while outside the main gate the wailing and moaning from the banshees became louder and louder. Khalen's guard seemed awestruck with the demonstration. Puzzled by the group around the rock and frustrated with the banshees, some of the guards began mocking the old hags. They put their neck scarves over their heads, used their swords as canes, and pretended to cry like babies."

"Olive Flametree and Chestnut Silvertwist, two *Raptorials* who Khalen thought he could trust, were in disguise and leading the banshees. They removed their disguises and came to the defense of the old hags. This made the guards look insensitive and arrogant and the *Raptorials* compared them to King Khalen. The crowd became very angry; the guards backed off and allowed the march to continue."

"As I stated," the monk continued, "it was already a gray stormy day; but, no doubt about it, King Odin added to the weather conditions. A powerful bolt of lightning cracked between the red and blue granite towers in the north and west of the city. Lightning circled the city between the other two granite towers several times until a major bolt struck the Meteoric Rock in the center of town scattering the butterfly-like messengers, many of them catching on fire. A shower of sparks and veins of electrical surges shot out of the rock.

I had been tracking a heretic in the area and a vein of electricity hit him; the surge was so strong it pulled him into Circle Six, making my job easy. The huge crack of thunder that followed stunned me. Of course, I gave thanks to God."

"Khalen and Lilliana were high up in the beige granite tower, the southern point of the city. I was curious as to what they would do, so I rushed to the tower. Terrifying screams echoed up the long stairwell from fair folk rushing for protection. Khalen and Lilliana peered over the ocean looking terrified."

"From the south, the direction of the oasis city of Finias, came four fire-breathing dragons," continued Rossal, his voice getting louder, "Their fire bolts traveled all the way to the Meteoric Rock that continued to send sparks deep into the sky, some so big that they collided with lightning bolts."

The knight went on, his voice returning to its usual pitch, "Khalen immediately recognized their leader; it was the sun goddess, Brighid, riding proudly on her favorite red dragon, Vestal. To her right was the wingless, but much larger golden dragon, Honeymeade. He was transporting King Odin, leader of the eastern city of air, Gorias. With him were his flying wolves and twin ravens followed by his wife, Queen Frigga, on their winged, eight-legged horse. They veered to their right toward the golden granite tower in the east and circled it."

"A gray, battle-worn dragon with blue webbed wings called Shaedow flew to Brighid's left. Lady Vivienne, the gentle queen of the water city, Murias, proudly flew on this beast with her long, flowing, silky blonde hair blowing in the wind. She had a stern look and veered to her left towards the western blue granite tower to circle it."

"Following the group in its original diamond-shaped formation was the skeletal dragon Shjeer. She was an imposing sight, I must say. Gywnn ap Nuud, the King of the Underworld rode this dragon. (The Underworld, for your information, is not a parallel world but a place where good folk wander and souls get lost.) Across the frame of the skeletal dragon was a sign that read: DOOMSDAY. The king carried a spear in one hand and a sword in the other. Shjeer lifted high in the sky over the red dragon and flew directly at the beige granite tower; Khalen and Lilliana watched in horror thinking that the beast was going to make a direct hit. Gwynn ap Nuud waved his sword at Khalen when his dragon pulled up, just missing the tower to begin a circling maneuver of the southern tower."

"Once Shjeer and the other two dragons became synchronized, Brighid made her grand entrance. The sun goddess spotted Khalen and Lilliana in the southern tower. On her dragon, Vestal, she dove at the tower, the red beast spewing flames and belching smoke. There was a near collision in the smoke with the skeletal dragon, Shjeer. Khalen and Lilliana looked on in horror; it appeared as if Vestal was going to drive the skeletal dragon into them when there was a near miss; they watched the red and gold underbelly of Vestal climbing over the tower. The sun goddess, dressed in red and gold armor to match her dragon, shook her fists at Khalen and Lilliana and then flew to the northern red granite tower."

"Brighid hovered there and held out her arms until all four dragons were synchronized." Rossal raised his voice again to a feverish pitch, "She suddenly raised her right fist, and all four dragons dove toward the Meteoric Rock, breathing fireballs and striking their target. A massive surge of sparks flew in every direction; a thick red glow of radiation emerged from the center of the city. The dragons, perfectly synchronized, flew over the rock one on top of each other with Vestal coming closest to hitting the Meteoric Rock. The dragons soaked up the electrical surges radiating from the rock like a crusty hunk of bread takes in thick gravy. They circled the city and then returned to their original towers for another attack."

Continuing in a raised pitch he went on, "Khalen and Lilliana left the beige tower, mounted their stallions, and headed towards the red granite tower, Khalen's control center for earth's electromagnetic energy. The black and white stallions raced through the city carrying their desperate king and queen, her black flowing hair and his pure white hair in stark contrast to each other. They passed the blue granite tower and sprinted along the river road to the red tower. King Odin spotted them and directed his raven's attention to the riders; they responded immediately. The

ravens dove at the riders and the stallions raced on faster than ever. Odin waved his arms and directed his wolves to chase them."

"The wolves were quick to reach the stallions and nipped at the horses tails until Khalen and Lilliana reached the red tower. At Khalen's command, the great wooden door of the tower opened; Lilliana and Khalen dismounted and entered. The wolves landed and faced off with the horses for a few tense moments. Odin sent a piercing whistle and the wolves returned to him to continue circling the gold tower, all of them now riding on Honeymeade, the golden dragon."

"The four dragons once again descended upon the center of the city," the knight's pitch softened considerably, "dropping tons of leaflets for the population to read. Odin's wounded butterfly army of sylphs and wind knots assisted the leaflets to land gently in the hands of everyone in the city. I thought they were really going to do something. The whole thing was a protest, **not** an attack."

"Khalen considered it an attack. He ran to the top of the red granite tower to his control panel connected to the meteorite. Despite the lightning bolts, his power source was fully functional. Khalen loaded the rock with a maximum potency; the rock was lethal from stored electricity. He sent a burst of power; all the leaflets burned so quickly they became balls of sparks. Odin responded with a burst of wind sending wind knots and sylphs to float off on the sparks in every direction. Dragons love excessive voltage, but the surge stunned them as well."

"Hovering over the western blue granite tower, Shaedow, the blue dragon carrying Lady Vivienne, was obviously confused from the ordeal and began to wander. She floated upwards in a daze. Turning a pale blue, she became a camouflage against the sky and drifted with the wind in an easterly direction. I saw Lady Vivienne collapse, passing out no doubt from a lack of oxygen."

"The huge golden dragon, Honeymeade, also struggled mightily. The beast surged towards the sun searching for relief; at an enormous speed he nearly collided with Shaedow. Unable to avoid the force, Shaedow spiraled downwards, out of control, crashing into the Lake of Manteith, throwing Lady Vivienne into deep water. She nearly drowned, but even with a torn wing, the blue dragon swept her up like a net bringing in fish, and carried the queen of Murias safely to shore."

"Back at the red granite tower more chaos ensued from the high voltage. Brighid screamed in terror when the tips of Vestal's red wings caught fire. The red dragon carried the sun goddess immediately toward the sea in the direction of their home in Finias, a trail of sparks following her. They landed in shallow water offshore of a small island on the coast. The water put out the fire but gave the dragon an awful shock. Brighid is a master healer; she attended to Vestal's burns."

"Honeymeade, the heaviest of all the beasts, reached a pinnacle in his quest for the sun and then lost his battle to remain airborne. He came spiraling towards the earth with King Odin still on board. Odin helped him as much as he could with a swirling wind, but Honeymeade crash-landed and slid onto the meteorite; it was still pulsing with heavy electromagnetic radiation. King Odin's ravens lifted the stunned king from Honeymeade's grasp just as they hit the big rock. They carried the king to safety atop the gold tower where he joined Frigga on their winged, eight-legged horse. Odin directed his ravens and wolves to circle Honeymeade, but they were helpless to stop Honeymeade from being electrocuted. His right leg was broken, stuck in a fissure in the rock, while the massive surge of energy struck his every nerve.

The skeletal dragon, Shjeer, had suffered no ill effects from the power surge. Circling the city with tremendous speed, she landed at the rock to help Honeymeade. The golden beast appreciated the gesture and belched a fireball into the rock. Gwyn ap Nuud had collapsed in Shjeer's saddle from the intense heat, but the skeletal dragon knew what she had to do. She lifted her mighty frame off the ground to hover over Honeymeade. Gently she attached her claws. After melting some rock to free Honeymeade's right leg, she slowly lifted the massive golden dragon off the rock and carried him gingerly to an open space. She set him down ever so gently.

The winged, eight-legged horse carried Odin and Frigga immediately to the wounded beast. Odin looked at the wound and then turned to the red tower. He waved his fist at Khalen who was standing in an open window."

"Khalen retreated to the inside of the tower where he turned off the power surge. The Meteoric Rock gave off a shower of gentle sparks."

"From the southwest, the sun broke through the clouds at the horizon. It was a brilliant sunset and captured everyone's attention. In the distance, they saw Vestal, her wings still smoking, returning to the city. Passing under a brilliant red cloud, the sun goddess flew directly to the dragons at the Meteoric Rock.

A master healer, Brighid assessed the injuries to Honeymeade and Gwynn ap Nuud. She revived the King of the Underworld and then applied a splint to Honeymeade's broken leg using the king's spear and sword.

Once again, Shjeer lifted Honeymeade to the sky. They flew off toward the oasis city of Finias. Odin and Frigga flew behind them. Brighid directed Vestal to fly east to find Lady Vivienne and Shaedow."

"Through this whole ordeal, I had not forsaken my duties of collecting heretics for Circle Six. The electrical surge from the Meteoric Rock created a whirlpool effect sending all these evil souls directly to Hell just like the one I had been tracking. I was free to follow Brighid and the red dragon."

"In no time, Vestal found their injured friends at the Lake of Manteith and joined them. Brighid collected some lavender that grew by the lake and applied a quick lavender treatment. Shaedow's normal blue color returned. Vestal helped her friend get airborne and they flew west to catch up with Shjeer and Honeymeade. Vestal flew underneath the golden dragon to provide support, although the skeletal dragon had never felt stronger. They had no further problems in their flight back to Finias. Gwynn ap Nuud and Lady Vivienne recovered physically, but their faces had changed. War has a similar effect on fair folk as it does to our species. That's how the war started."

"Your recount of the battle was overwhelming," said the minister. "I have no sense of time."

"Don't even think about time," said Rossal. "It's a relative thing anyway, something I rarely consider."

"What else has happened?" asked the minister.

"Khalen declared victory in battle," said Rossal. "Days upon days of attacks have followed. Brighid has an army of fifty dragons that live at her palace in the oasis city. Every day at least one fire breathing dragon flies from Finias to Falias to scorch the city. The polished granite towers of Falias are turning black with soot, as are the roads and everything else. Heat from the dragons' breath alone has made the roads in the city impassable. Magnificent trees along the river parkway have lost their leaves."

"Trolls toss heavy rocks over the walls of the city and Khalen's royal guards are powerless to stop them. Many residents became sympathetic to the Raptorials and moved away. Khalen used work crews with humans to try to clean up the mess for a while, but abandoned that plan. The beleaguered king ultimately issued an order for Falias to be uninhabited. The most solid city and jewel of the earth is now closed. Khalen announced yesterday that no one deserves to live there."

"Counter attacks have been conducted with Khalen sending power surges to the other three major cities. For a brief period, he disabled the blue beam protecting the oasis city of Finias from the desert heat. To aggravate Lady Vivienne, his surges created rough ocean currents and a relatively low tidal wave on Murias. He paid Odin back with unpredictable weather patterns for Gorias. Gwynn Ap Nuud experienced numerous earthquakes in the Underworld. No deaths have been attributed to the war, but there's been no peace."

The knight paused a minute and then added, "No attacks have been made on Fairy Knowe because of you. Every leader wants to know about you. They want to know what Khalen knows. Since he is outnumbered, they believe that he will succumb to their pressure. Khalen is really in control and that's because of you."

"In addition to fairies bickering with each other, every human soul entering this world, both good and bad, has taken up the fight to have you released. Chaos is everywhere."

"What is the status of my son's health?"

"I have reluctantly held back this grim news in the hope of some change. A doppelganger has attached himself to your son; death is near," said Rossal. "The Holy Nail is in a small wooden box and tucked away. It is of no use to him. I pray for him all the time as you do. We will pray together before I return to Circle Six," and they did.

CHAPTER 13

THE LAST BATTLE

minister Kirk had a lot to think about; the parallel worlds of Hell and the chaos in this world brought about by his capture was overwhelming enough, but foremost in his mind was the news about his son's imminent passing. He continued to try to communicate with Kirk Jr. through prayer. Finally, he received the visit he had been expecting; Hugues de Payens appeared before him in a somber mood.

"God be with you," said Hugues. "Are you staying optimistic?"

"God be with you also," replied the minister. "I fear you bring sad news about my son."

"Your son spent his last hour standing by your grave across the field before you," said Hugues. "He was a fine man in life. Without having your gift of sight, it was hard for him to understand you. I saw the doppelganger leave his body and head directly to Khalen's war room. Your son thanked God for the opportunity to join you. He collapsed and died."

"I understand," said the minister. "Can you give me the full story?"

"It was a foggy, damp day. I looked across the field to your grave and your church as I often do," said the knight. "The church was still boarded up, looking many years older. Through the fog, I could see there was still no gravestone. Your son walked up to your grave and turned towards you in this tree.

I asked Godfrey to patrol my gateway and travelled through the portal below to be with your son. I stood next to him."

"After a period of silence, he spoke to you, 'Dear earthly father, this will be my last visit to your grave. I soon will know the afterlife. My sixty years on earth is ending. Fairies have not been as aggressive since your passing. In that regard, you have done us a great service. We still believe there could be trouble. I hope you forgive me; your book will never be published. There is too much potential danger; fairies will never tolerate their secrets being told. You talked about the double-men; my double-man has probably already left me. Had I had your gift of second sight, I could have understood you better."

"He wiped away his tears, looked out at the fog over the field and said, 'I remember you telling me about the first time you saw the fairy queen: It was a perfect spring day. A group of small fairies, in pastel colors of pink, blue, yellow, and green, danced in a circle around their queen. She was dressed in a white lace gown and danced in a counter circle to her court. A large pink ribbon bow circled underneath her bodice and flowed around her. She extended her arms over her head holding a bouquet of mixed daisies, while a crown of the same pastel flowers adorned her silky black hair. Her smile spread joy to all who gazed upon her beauty."

"He paused for a moment and continued, 'It still puzzles me as to how such a gentle creature could be a threat to us all. So as the fog blocks out my view of Fairy Knowe I think about this enigma."

"The doppelganger left his body. His spirit looked at me, puzzled at seeing a knight and probably thinking about the Holy Nail. Robert was frightened; I put my hand on his right shoulder. The bright, protective, white light that surrounds all souls at death engulfed him. We crossed into this parallel world. I was happy to be there with him to share the moment."

"He did not need my protection, for an angel greeted us when we crossed through. 'You will wait here for a short time,' said the angel. 'Your soul is strong and you are destined to the outer universe, probably Heaven."

"The angel left and your son looked around and then looked at me."

"Are you here for my protection?' he asked."

"I told him that I came for that purpose, but that he was under God's protection until the time of decision. I told him about your incarceration in this tree; he already knew as much. I told him I was your friend. Suddenly we saw thousands of souls heading toward us. This was nothing like I had ever seen before. An angry soul spoke to your father."

"You must join the fight,' he demanded. 'Fairies are trying to extract your father's soul. This would mean doom for him and for all of humankind. You still have a free will and can choose to fight. We need you to be our leader."

"I had to return to my post for fear that Godfrey was being over-whelmed with the masses. I left your son with the mob."

"It was an awful night. All souls in this world were angered by your son's passing. They taunted the fairies with one ghostly spectacle after another. Lightning flashed all night long, but there was no thunder, only groans of torture and madness. Evil souls were much harder to control making our jobs at the gateways very difficult. We fought them all night long."

"Sunrise brought relief to the fairies," continued the knight. "The army of souls diminished in the light of day; cheers came from within the palace built into this hill."

"Your son was last seen by Gondemar," continued Hugues, "the other monk you've not yet met. Gondemar patrols the violent offenders of Circle Seven. Your son told him he wanted to visit you and would stop at nothing to free you from this horror. While they were talking, Gondemar had hold of an evil one that constantly interrupted them, claiming he did not deserve a punishment in Hell, that his murderous crime was sanctioned by a holy man. Your son suddenly grabbed the evil one and flung him into Hell. That's all I have for now."

"I am proud of my son," said the minister. "He is, I fear, in great danger."

"I agree," said Hugues.

Interrupting them, the monk Rossal rushed to Hugues' side.

"Rossal," said Hugues, "Only one of us should be away from our post at any given time. This is not the time to tell your tale of Circle Six."

"I pray that you forgive me, my leader," said Rossal. "An attack on Fairy Knowe by the Raptorials and Dissidents is about to unfold. Every human soul from around this world is poised to create chaos in the area. Kirk Jr. is leading the fight. We must return to our posts."

The two knights quickly returned to their respective circles. Minister Kirk heard Khalen and Lilliana coming into the circle garden at the base of his tree.

"I have never heard and seen so many ghosts," said Lilliana.

"They have been gathering in huge numbers since the death of the minister's son," said Khalen. "Reportedly, Robert E. Kirk Jr. has become their leader. I have a plan to capture him. Perhaps then they will leave us alone."

"What do you have in mind?" asked Lilliana.

"I captured his father inside a gateway," explained Khalen. "I will capture him in the same way."

"Another captured soul would also show our adversaries that your skills have become more powerful," added Lilliana. "That alone could stop the fighting."

"All of this ghostly activity has everyone more afraid of an attack," said Khalen. "Violence could erupt and destroy our peaceful world. Their fear is unjustified; the family does not want Kirk's book published. They want the minister's legend to die. I have to quell this uprising."

"I agree," said Lilliana. "No one would believe your report about the family turning their back on the minister," said Lilliana. "Chaos is brewing."

"I know what to do," said Khalen.

At that moment Beetle Willowleaf and Thorn Cornembers, two of Khalen's finest guards came rushing up the path to the garden circle.

"King Khalen, we have captured a *Raptorial*," exclaimed Willowleaf.

"He was caught with thousands of locusts in a wagon across the field," added Cornembers.

"We think he was waiting for others to attack Fairy Knowe," said Willowleaf.

"What is his name and where is he from?" asked Khalen.

"You know him, sir," said Cornembers. "He went on two of the missions to Hell; he is Chestnut Silvertwist, from the woodlands."

"The *Raptorials* are hard-headed," said Khalen. "Take him to the middle of the field and put chains on him."

"That would be torture," said Lilliana. "For woodland folk, being out in an open field is like putting desert folk under water. He would be terrified."

"We must make an example of him," said Khalen. "His accomplices will come to his aid and the lot of them will face this evening's haunt. The ghosts will have a target for their nightly rampage. Silvertwist will be the bait for my trap."

"We will do as you say, my king," said Willowleaf.

"Place a sign on him," said Khalen. "Have it read: **The War Is Over -- Go Home!**"

Willowleaf and Cornembers did as instructed. They made a wooden platform and tied Silvertwist to a post in the middle. Horses dragged the platform to the middle of the field. Willowleaf then had the horses drag

iron chains to surround him on the platform, essentially chaining him to the post. They made four signs facing in all directions to deliver Khalen's message to go home.

Silvertwist was defiant, "Our laws serve only the king," he shouted. "These iron chains are cruel. You are not concerned about a human invasion because you have the soul. Your king does not care for my immortality and me getting a soul. We will fight you for the soul. You will not get away with this. Our passion for eternal life is greater than for serving you."

Beetle Willowleaf countered, "King Khalen took you to Hell in good faith to see what could happen when you get a soul. We know that love conquers all, and he loves you. Fighting will not get you what you desire. This act to end the war is necessary. It hurts King Khalen more than it does you. You must follow our code and honor the king."

"He is your king, not mine," said a defiant Silvertwist. "He is putting us all in danger. The world will know the minister's secrets and come for him. If Khalen knows what he is doing, then why has no one received a soul? I will tell you why; he is giving it only to the folk he likes."

"You have dishonored our king and must be punished," said Thorn Cornembers. "Make this easy for yourself; tell us who you are working with."

"I work alone," said Chestnut.

"Is Olive Flametree in on this?" asked Beetle.

"Olive would not be a part of this," said Thorn, placing his hand on Beetle's shoulder. "She is my friend."

"Set me free," shouted Silvertwist. "Do not leave me out here in the open. Have some mercy on me."

"You should have thought this through," stated Beetle. "You were going to set those locusts on Queen Lilliana's gardens. You are lucky we are not putting you in a box with them."

"Have a good day and night," said Thorn. "When your friends come by, tell them to go home and stop this war."

"When the ghosts come by this evening," added Willowleaf, "try singing them a woodland tune to help them sleep."

Willowleaf and Cornembers left Silvertwist on his platform. The woodland fairy cried and wailed like it was the end of the earth. All day long, he continued to go between fits of crying and shouting. On the other side of Fairy Knowe, Olive Flametree, Regina Spideroaster, and Sneaky McLittle, had mounted an attack using thousands of worms. They heard Silvertwist's cries for help. While they wanted to help him, they decided to stay with their plan and hoped his cries would rally folk everywhere to his aid. Crowds of good folk assembled in the field.

While the fair folk were busy with battle preparations, Robert E. Kirk Jr. organized all available souls in the mock cemetery.

Before sunset, Khalen and Lilliana rode their stallions to visit Silver-twist and to make an announcement. A huge crowd had gathered and chanted their disapproval of Silvertwist's treatment. Nevertheless, the king and queen rode to the platform with their heads high. They dis-mounted and stepped up to their captive.

"Silvertwist," said Khalen, "You do not have to remain here through the night. Who are your accomplices and what is your plan?"

No response came from the woodland fairy.

"You will receive a fair judgement," continued Khalen. "I will end the war. With this kind of behavior, you would end up in Hell once you receive a soul. Disobedience is not to be tolerated. You need to cooperate with me."

"You care only for *Tolerants*," screamed Silvertwist. "The proof is in me being tortured in the middle of a field and sickened with iron chains."

The crowd jeered and gave shouts to release the woodland fairy. Kha-len and Lilliana rode back to Fairy Knowe as the sun began to set. As they rode away, they could hear Silvertwist's voice above the crowd.

"Beauty is freedom," shouted Chestnut. "We must use any means pos-sible to achieve our own immortality. Humans do not deserve such a gift. You have captured me but *Raptorials* will stay united with *Dissidents* in the battle for the human soul."

Kirk Jr. and his army waited patiently for the last rays of the sun. A ground fog settled in over the field; the army had their instructions. Fair folk were very reluctant to leave poor Silvertwist alone. His crying was pathetic and leaving him there for the ghosts made them feel horrible; but the crowd did not want to face the ghosts either. Fair folk were angry, yet sad and anxious, a complete emotional mess. They crowded around Chestnut Silvertwist and tried feverishly to free him from chains made of iron. It was a futile effort and a demonstration of power for Khalen to apply such a punishment.

A ground fog began to cover the field. It was a perfect cover; in si-lence Kirk Jr.'s army circled them. Not one fairy had realized the onslaught until Kirk Jr. suddenly appeared before Silvertwist.

"This is your Hell," shouted Kirk Jr. "I will haunt you until my father's soul is released or until your mind explodes. Blood will be on the hands of your king should my father continue to be imprisoned." To his army he shouted, "Let's give them a taste of Hell and make them wish they'd never heard of man's soul."

The good folk were panic-stricken. They ran in every direction, screaming and crying. The ghosts fed on their fear like sharks in the water. Maddening screams and terrifying faces chased the fairies from all sides. Silvertwist was scared out of his wits. His eyes looked like they were going to pop.

To add to the terror of the crowd, Kirk Jr. taunted the chained fairy, while his army of ghosts unleashed their anger on other fairies now trapped in the field. Running helter-skelter in every direction and into each other, fairy folk screamed and cried for help. The apparitions constantly drove them back to Silvertwist; he was the most terrorized of all of them. The woodland fairy pleaded for anyone to get Khalen to help him. Shouts to end Silvertwist's torture and their own nightmare clearly made their way to Khalen, now observing the ordeal from his palace.

Across the hill on the opposite side of Fairy Knowe were Olive Flametree and her entourage. Armed with about a million worms, this group was delighted about the distraction in the field. Olive directed the party to attack while the ghosts were busy.

They ascended a small tree at the base of the hill to get to the forest canopy. Regina Spideroaster linked a net across the top of the trees. This allowed the smaller leprechauns to form a chain all the way from the base of the hill to look down on Lilliana's private garden. The plan worked perfectly. Only Minister Kirk was aware of the leprechauns passing along the worms over the forest canopy and dropping them on the garden.

King Khalen focused completely on the battle. He finally ordered Beetle Willowleaf to go to Silvertwist and pretend to give him aid, until he could give Kirk Jr. a message. Willowleaf was terrified of the ghosts but maintained his focus and sympathies on Silvertwist.

"Suffer no longer, Silvertwist," said Willowleaf. "Your ordeal is over."

Robert E. Kirk Jr. rushed at Khalen's guard making Willowleaf tremble before him. "This fairy will remain here until you bring me news of my father's release."

"I will take you to my King," said Willowleaf. "He has the power to release the minister."

"Fellow spirits cease your haunts," commanded Kirk Jr, and the field cleared. "Silvertwist must remain in chains," he continued, "until I have seen evidence of my father's freedom. When I'm convinced this is not a trick, the ghosts will leave."

"It is a deal," said Willowleaf. "Silvertwist will remain here for the time being."

Poor Silvertwist never felt more alone; he cried and wailed like never before as he watched Willowleaf and his tormenter cross the field and climb the hill.

Upon reaching the circle garden, Kirk Jr. stopped abruptly; for in front of him was an open portal, a view to his father's grave across from Doon Hill. It was like a window, a tunnel in space. Through the gateway, the son saw the image of his father in his nightgown, his last memory of him when he was alive and when he appeared at his sister's christening.

"Go to him," said Khalen standing behind the tree. "I want to end this madness. Your father's soul is about to return to his grave in your world to complete the farewell he never had."

Kirk Sr. watched in horror from above as his son took the bait; he did not realize he was looking at a projected image. Stepping into the gateway, a vortex of red light waves captured Kirk Jr. He was helpless to do anything. Within moments, beams of light emerged from the gateway and bore a hole into the tree. Kirk Jr.'s soul traveled along those beams until he locked into the cellular structure of the tree near his father.

The beams of light boring into the tree were so brilliant that the entire area around Fairy Knowe, including the field, was lit up like daylight. Worms were everywhere; they covered the palace devouring everything. Hordes of them had already moved to the open field looking for food; they were closing in on Silvertwist.

The army of ghosts suddenly realized they were without a leader. They fled from the area of the mock cemetery to avoid capture. Silvertwist was very close to going mad when a bolt of energy akin to a lightning strike hit the worms crawling on his platform. A thunderous snap made him think for a moment that he was dead; he discovered his chains were broken and he was free from the post.

The booming voice of Khalen projected over the area, "Go home, Silvertwist," he shouted, his voice echoing. "Your chains have been shattered. The war is over. My power has grown. I have captured a new soul. He is Robert E. Kirk Jr., the minister's son. Be patient and respect my power. I have the power of life and death; and a soul you may one day acquire. Spread the news; the war is over."

Silvertwist never stopped running until he reached his home in the woods. Khalen apprehended Flametree, Spideroaster, and Sneaky McLittle. He placed them in the dungeon for the remainder of the night with many of the worms. At sunrise, thousands of birds descended on Fairy Knowe for breakfast. Despite the mess and destruction, Khalen released his prisoners to show compassion and start the healing process.

News spread fast about Khalen's accomplishment as well as his compassion for the protesters. War had ended.

From deep inside the cellular structure of the old pine young Kirk reunited with his father, "Father, are you here?"

"You fought valiantly, my son," said the father.

"I fought for you as long as I could."

"We must pray together," said the father. "I tried to warn you in your dreams."

"I did have one dream with you, father. I did not follow your ministry. Now I've failed you."

"We have been captured, my son, but we have not yet failed mankind. Let's pray that together we'll be stronger."

CHAPTER 14

THOUGHT MANIPULATORS

Word spread very quickly about Khalen's achievements. He had quelled the reign of terror from the ghosts and captured another soul. His potential power to control every soul demanded respect. His demonstration had been impressive, especially the shattering of iron (which was not actually iron, but an imitation).

By releasing Chestnut Silvertwist and the worm brigade, Khalen earned the admiration of everyone as a fair leader with compassion for all. He attempted to convince fair folk from every region that he had their best interests at heart. Chestnut Silvertwist received an honor for remaining calm in the presence of ghosts. At a festival in Silvertwist's honor, the woodland fairy became a member of Khalen's Royal Guard. Lilliana planted a chestnut tree where his ordeal took place.

Khalen convinced the other reluctant leaders that no attack was forthcoming, and that the minister's family was powerless. He forged an agreement with Odin, Brighid, and Lady Vivienne to allow him to pursue an image change through poets and politicians. Fairy tales would prove how love conquers all.

There was no pressure on Khalen to share his technology and he had as much time as he needed, provided there was no threat of invasion. Khalen swore to the *Fairy Code* that he was to be trusted.

After the celebrations ended, calm returned to Fairy Knowe. Reunited in captivity, the two Kirks had each other.

"I can't imagine how awful this incarceration has been for you," commented the son.

"I've missed you and our family so much," said the father. "My memories of our life together have been my focus, the mainstay for my survival. The fairy king has been relentless in his efforts to break me down. Whenever he attacks, I shift my focus to block out everything he does. As long as you use this strategy my son, hope will remain alive."

"You must have been very lonely," commented the son.

"Did you see the knights on this hill?" asked the father.

"I did see them. They never offered their help to me in any battle."

"You rejected their gift of the Holy Nail. They are the original Knights Templar and are responsible for guarding the gates of Hell. It's their job to send evil souls to their destination and prevent any escape. I receive visits from them from time to time. They tell me tales to keep me company, providing they're not away from their posts very long. One of their ancestors gave you a Holy Nail."

At that moment Rossal, the monk, arrived outside the tree.

"My condolences younger Kirk," said Rossal, "you fought well and deserved a much better outcome. Sadly and prayerfully, I bring greetings to you from the fairy world. I am Rossal, Knight Templar and monk."

"It's an honor to meet you Rossal," said the son. "My father just told me about your mission. I only wish I could have fought like a knight to get my father released."

King Khalen is savvy," said Rossal. "He baited you into the gateway and snatched you with his light beam. To help your father pass time, we have been telling him our tales. I guard Circle Six and must be quick in the telling of my tale and return to my post. I hope you understand."

"My son has been apprised of your tales," said Kirk Sr. "Please tell us yours."

"Here I go then."

It was a still evening; the air seemed heavy, almost lifeless, if you know what I mean, Rossal began. Woodland creatures were restless and fidgety. A pair of heretics, two politicians arguing about their failure to keep a religious group under their control, ventured down the path from the gateway below us. I grabbed them by the scruffs of their necks and held them above Circle Six. One soul shriveled up and was sucked into the hole.

'You heretics are the worst,' I said. 'You twist logic and thrive by using people's fears to stay in power to get what **you** want.'

The second soul was then sucked into the hole. Their disruption caused more restlessness for the small animals. Khalen came up the main path followed by Beetle Willowleaf and Chestnut Silvertwist, the same woodland fairy who had been chained in the field. The two of them are good friends now, but back then, they were on opposite sides and arguing about their turtles. Willowleaf apparently had a river cooter and Silvertwist had a wood turtle. Can you imagine arguing about turtles when you're moments away from going to Hell?"

Anyway, the three of them stopped in front of circle 6. Khalen looked at me and I said to him, 'I pray one day you'll find permanent residence down there.'

He looked away from me. They held hands to form a circle and spun around seven times. Like a mist, they entered into the circle. I looked in and for the first time things became visible. I could follow them, see them, and hear everything. It was like an open window.

Howling wind through trees, and thousands of glowing eyes, all different sizes, surrounded them until they landed on a forest floor. They broke their circle and looked around.

'That was powerful,' said Chestnut, 'I am glad we are in a forest. I love the forest. I feel at home here.'

However, the forest was full of creatures, none of them from the forest. Scorpions, rattlesnakes, and black widow spiders crawled on the forest floor. The trees were full of vultures. The fairies started walking towards what looked like a small creek. Souls were there trying to drink while fighting off these desert creatures.

Disgusted by what they saw, the fairies followed the creek out of the forest only to end up on a street in a rundown city. Souls came pouring out of the alleys followed by panthers and hyenas. I saw pythons crawling through windows; screams came from inside old, dilapidated buildings.

Continuing down the street, the fairies walked out of town and into a desert. Rats and cockroaches swarmed around them in a circle of palm trees; an oasis I presume. Two-headed Hell hounds dragged in several souls and offered them up to the rats and cockroaches; they were consumed by these vermin from the city that were somehow in the desert?"

Finally, the fairy folk crossed the desert only to return to the forest. From high in the trees, I heard a voice say, 'I'm your leader. Forget what you know about reality. Trust me and do as I say. I know what's best for you.'

'Nothing in this world makes sense,' stated Chestnut.

'Their leader violated common sense rules of the universe for power,' said Khalen. 'In life, he convinced everyone to follow his way of thinking; he changed things for the sake of change. He had enormous power but did not think things through. He now leads other souls of like mind.'

They joined hands, continued Rossal, and in a straight-line lead by Khalen, they travelled back through the windy tunnel to stand before me.

'As a knight,' said Khalen to me, 'you fought for religious reasons. How did you know your fight was for the right reasons?'

'Religious freedom is personal,' said I to him. 'It's important for the development of the soul, and free will. Heretics manipulate others to force their will on others. When they violate common sense laws for peaceful coexistence, they rightfully find their home here.'

He looked through me as if I wasn't there. Willowleaf and Silver-
twist walked away and started arguing about their turtles again.

As soon as Rossal finished his tale, Gondemar, the other monk, showed up to tell his.

"I'm sorry to interrupt you," apologized the second monk. "Something very unusual has been taking place below you in the garden. While the fairies have had one party after another, today's party is very unusual and I thought you should watch them. They are escorting one human folk after another to the garden. Never before has Khalen allowed human folk into this garden for a royal celebration."

"I see them," said Kirk Jr. "They have musicians, dancers, and jugglers."

"Fairies are serving them food and wine and treating them like royalty," added Gondemar.

"Good day," said Rossal, "I've just finished my tale anyway."

"Wonderful," commented Gondemar, "I can tell the minsters my tale about the violence in Circle Seven."

"My dear Gondemar," said Rossal, "I pray that you see the merriment and festivities below us. The ministers Kirk are certainly more interested in watching the party than hearing your tale."

"Is that true ministers Kirk?" asked Gondemar.

"We would love to hear your tale," said the father.

"You see that my fellow monk," said Gondemar to Rossal.

"But, the festivities below are rather peculiar," said Kirk Sr. "I've never seen one of our species in the garden."

"This is a first," agreed Rossal. "I'm interested in seeing what happens too.

"I guess my tale can wait for another day," said Gondemar.

"What is that black box next to the King's chair?" asked the younger Kirk.

"It is some form of power device," explained Rossal.

"It has many different effects on the human mind," added Gondemar. "Every human brought to this world has been brainwashed from whatever comes from that box. They have no understanding of the soul and believe they are a subservient species. It's like their free will has been paralyzed."

"The sad thing is," added Rossal, "they're all very happy, or at least think they're happy."

"Why doesn't Khalen take their souls?" asked Kirk Jr.

"These are weak, underdeveloped souls," explained Rossal. "He wants only strong souls, like both of yours, to give his folk."

"I can see Hugues at Circle Nine, and he is not happy with us. I should have waited at my circle until you returned to yours, Rossal. Pray for me," said Gondemar. "I've shown a lack of self-discipline unbecoming a knight. I will tell you my tale another time, dear ministers. The witch in it is very funny."

Both knights returned quickly to their posts.

At the garden party, the humans were enjoying themselves. Kirk Sr. noticed that the humans did not talk to each other. They ate and drank and talked to the fair folk, but simply smiled at each other, acknowledging their happiness.

Each person took turns sitting next to Khalen and Lilliana. Khalen adjusted some knobs on his black box after talking to each person. The ministers could hear the conversations and they were all the same. The laborers were happy to be recognized and grateful to the fair folk for caring for them and giving them everything they needed. None of them had any worries; all were grateful for what they received. The party ended, but Lilliana and Khalen remained in the garden.

"The human mind is so easy to manipulate," boasted Khalen.

"You have them so well trained," said Lilliana. "The humans did not speak to each other."

"They know their place," said Khalen. "I am developing a plan to change our image in their world. I want their relatives to love us the same. I will convince humans in our parallel world to believe we are special, that we will take care of them providing they keep our relationship private. They will treasure our interventions and never speak to each other about us. A private trust will be started in childhood and if broken would bring them ridicule, bad luck, and even worse. Everyone will love us; we will be adored. The will to fight us will be lost. We will become a major source for childhood imagination and adult fantasy. The fear they have for us now will turn to love."

"We will conquer all," commented Lilliana. "That is truly brilliant, my love. What are your plans to accomplish this?"

"My plan started just after the minister's death, 1692 in his world. I connected with an elder chap, a Frenchman, Charles Perrault. He was very receptive to making a collection of folk tales. His collection, the *Tales of Mother Goose*, was well written and published in 1697. Perrault was seventy years of age; an elderly man delivering my message gave it more credibility; he died at age seventy-five adding to the total effect. His tales, not well received at first as you can imagine, planted my seeds. His book, started as folk tales changed to fairy tales, has now taken a hold in the hearts and imaginations of humans everywhere."

"I am so proud of this accomplishment," he continued. "There is more good news. Since the time of Perrault (over a hundred years in their time) two brothers, Jacob and Wilhelm Grimm are continuing the tales. Children love them. We will be seen as loving, magical beings (as we are) for centuries to come. Our image is changing; they no longer fear us. They love us. Human folk want to believe our fantasized image is real to hold on to a childhood fantasy. They will not talk about us to each other for the fear of embarrassment and being teased."

"That is wonderful," said Lilliana. "We earn their trust as children and they will love us for their whole life. What about the minister's book?" asked Lilliana. "Could that information still cause us problems?"

"No one will take the book seriously after the tales have been released. I have total confidence that it will cause no alarm whatsoever; I will arrange for its printing. People will look at it like another fairy tale. This is a perfect time in history to prey upon the human imagination to earn their trust and love."

"How will you do it?"

"Colors, sounds, and fragrances all affect a chemical (oxytocin) in the human mind. I can use the earth's power, the electromagnetic energy that flows like rivers around the globe with waves of red energy to connect with the oxytocin in their minds. We can influence human fear, temptations, and creativity; their basic thoughts are easy to manipulate."

"The gentle spirits of our world," continued Khalen, "those that resemble butterflies, flowers, and the like will meet them at every corner where there are moments of vulnerability, wishful moments when humans are willing to listen. They will be seduced into wanting more of us until they are under our control. They will not suspect a thing and take full credit for their creativity. I will bring joy to their world. When their soul is part of our DNA, they will have brought joy to us."

"Father," said Kirk Jr., "do you think that mankind can survive this?"

"We must pray that something goes wrong with their plan," said the father. All we can do is pray and hold on."

CHAPTER 15

A Focus on Violence

Gondemar, the other monk turned knight, was quick to leave his post as soon as the fairies' party was over.

"Ministers Kirk, I'm happy to tell you my tale now. Are you as eager to receive it?"

"My dear, Gondemar," said the elder Kirk, "We are very troubled at what we just witnessed. The fairy king has a plan to convert the children of man to love fairies."

"His goal is to make our world love them before he takes our souls," said Kirk Jr. "Can he do that?"

"All we can do is pray," said Gondemar. "The power of prayer is our only weapon against them. With prayer, we have two great advantages: our species far outnumbers theirs, and the energy and strength behind the power of prayer frightens them. It frightens them because they have no power over it. As long as one soul is praying, we can defeat this enemy."

"We know you're eager to tell your tale," said Kirk Sr. "After we hear it, we'll pray for their failure."

"I hope my tale cheers you up a bit," said the knight.

"The reality of violent offenders going to Hell cheers me up already," said Kirk Jr.

"It humors me to think of fairies' down there," said the father. "Sometimes the situations are funny, like when it snowed on the day they learned about the circle with lust."

"We've had many good laughs at them," said Gondemar. "It was a mild fall afternoon when I had my experience, the kind

121

of afternoon made for reading my Bible, taking a nap, and waking up to witness God's beauty."

He paused for a moment to say a quiet prayer and then began his tale.

On that day, colorful autumn leaves swirled around the garden below; a small whirlpool of leaves circled around the baby owl in its birdbath. Regina Spideroaster, the witch who works closely with Baba Yaga, flew into the garden on a flying stick. She startled the baby owl; the mother owl dove to its protection. Regina cackled and with a burst of speed, she flew around the owls, adding to the whirlpool effect of the leaves. This excited the witch. As she got faster and faster, every leaf from the forest became part of a whirlpool, now looking like a small tornado. Suddenly the crazy witch darted out of the swirling leaves, flying in a haphazard manner, cutting through the leaves, and ultimately dove towards the mother owl sheltering her baby.

'I love the wind and the leaves in my hair,' shouted the crazed witch.

The mother owl rose up to defend her baby and attacked Regina knocking her off her stick and into a pile of leaves. The witch thought it was funny and cackled hysterically.

Petal Hailfrost and Honey Driftsfur obviously heard the witch and came running up the main path to see what was going on. The two fairies began laughing when they saw Regina acting crazy in the pile of leaves.

'Can we join you?' asked Honey.

'This looks like so much fun,' added Petal.

'I want to keep the leaves swirling,' shouted Regina. 'They're slowing down. Catch me if you can,' she added as she found her stick and took off again.

The two friends went airborne and chased Regina all around the garden, flying through the leaves, around the tree, into the woods, and all over Fairy Knowe. The fairies laughed; Regina cackled and the mother owl transported her baby out of the garden.

Up the path came Lilliana and Khalen on their horses. Petal and Honey, focused totally on catching Regina, never saw Khalen until Regina's foot caught the king in the middle of his back; he fell off his horse sending Regina into a pile of leaves in the circle garden.

Lilliana dismounted and helped Khalen to his feet; he was not injured. Petal landed on the witch and held her down, the witch cackling the whole time. Honey followed her and took the opportunity to start tickling Regina. The nasty old witch farted. Oh my goodness, what a fart she made.

Khalen and Lilliana started laughing hysterically as Honey and Petal let the witch go and backed away quickly bumping into Khalen and Lilliana.

'It sounds like Regina had sweet milk for breakfast,' commented Khalen.

'What is the definition of a lively witch?' asked Lilliana with a smile on her face.

'I do not know,' replied Honey.

'It is a witch, who can jump in the air and fart three times before hitting the ground,' said Lilliana. They all laughed, not expecting the queen to say 'fart.'

'What's the definition of a mean witch?' asked Regina.

'Tell us,' replied Petal. "Your speech is so uncouth.'

'It's a witch who farts on a campfire while her sisters are stirring the stew.' She paused and then added with her eyes growing larger, 'I burnt their tongues and singed their eyelashes.'

They all laughed; even I chuckled at that one, said Gondemar, chuckling again at his story.

'Where in Hell are we going today, King Khalen?' asked Honey.

Gondemar chuckled again at this, but the ministers had no reaction. *I'm sorry I digressed a bit, said the knight. We find these fairies a little amusing at times. I'll get more into going to Hell, now.*

'Let us walk to Circle Seven,' said Khalen. 'I am not going with you today. Lilliana and I discussed this; I would be a threat to the violent souls in Circle Seven's three inner circles. I do not want to take the chance that one of them could lash out at me and accidentally harm one of you. Lilliana will lead Honey and Regina on this mission. You must not stay in one place too long. Stay together and you will learn a lot.'

Petal gave Honey a hug. Regina said, 'As long as Honey's with me, what could go wrong?'

'Everything could go wrong,' said Petal. 'You are so bad. The devil down there may just keep you even though you do not have a soul.'

They all looked at me, said Gondemar. I nodded my head in agreement.

'As spooky as this Knight is,' said Petal, 'he knows I am right. The devil would love you, Regina.'

*Lilliana buttoned up her white leather jacket, put on her white
leather gloves and said, 'I am ready. Let us see what Circle Seven has
to offer. I hope it smells better than Circle One.'*

*'Don't blame that on me,' said Regina with a smile. 'I didn't do
anything down there.'*

*'You better not fart in this circle,' said Khalen. 'The flames down
there could set off an explosion.'*

Gondemar laughed aloud and then continued, *they all chuckled again and proceeded as if they were going to a picnic. The three
locked hands and spun so fast that they lost their grip and fell on their
backsides. They got to their feet, rejoined in a circle and off they went
into the pinhole. I watched closely knowing I was going to see things
down there.*

*What surprised me though was the burst of heat from their entry.
I jumped back quickly, not expecting to feel anything. When I looked
back in the hole, I saw total darkness; I thought I had lost my chance
to see them until sparks began to fly. Some of the sparks hit the witch
and she screamed. Light emerged around them and they went into an
open space with three concentric circles below them. There was a red
one on the outside, burnt orange in the middle and yellowish orange at
the center. I could clearly hear them talking.*

*'These are my kind of colors,' shouted Regina. 'I feel dizzy and
light like burnt butterfly wings. This is great. Are we going to go
through all the colors?'*

Just then the witch broke grip with them, said Gondemar. *She
flew off and cackled, just as she did in the leaves.*

*'I won't like Hell in the future, so I'll enjoy it now,' shouted Re-
gina.*

*Her voice echoed and that seemed to excite her even more. Lilliana
and Honey kept their grip and flew after the witch.*

*'The river below us smells like blood,' said Lilliana. 'It is making
the witch crazy. We have to get control of her.'*

'I have captured her before; I can do it again,' said Honey.

*'She will not be drawn to the orange circle,' said Lilliana. 'Souls
from suicide missions go there. Nor will she go to the yellow circle.
Those souls have committed violence against God. She knows nothing
about that. The violent offenders must be giving her a thrill. She has
a very wicked streak in her. She is now heading directly to the river of
blood.'*

'Do you see the large tree by the river?' asked Honey.

'I see it,' replied Lilliana.

'Go to that tree and I will bring Regina to you. I know what I am doing.'

'You are so brave, Honey. I will meet you at the tree.'

Honey let go of Lilliana and darted off toward Regina. In flight, she began to mimic the witch, much as she had done with Petal back at the garden. Regina looked at her and shouted, 'Catch me if you can.'

'Regina,' called Honey, 'I have another joke; I want to tell it to you.'

'I don't want to hear it. I'm having too much fun,' said the witch.

'I thought you were my friend,' said Honey.

'What's your stupid joke?' asked Regina.

'Do you see the big tree by the river of blood?' asked Honey.

'What river of blood?' asked the witch.

'Look down to your right. Do you see Lilliana trapped near a tree by the river of blood? There are violent offenders all around her. We must save her or we will not ever be able to get out of here. Be my friend and help me,' pleaded Honey.

'I see her. What am I doing? I do not know what came over me. We must save her and save ourselves. How can you think of a joke at a time like this, Honey? Take my hand.'

Regina took Honey's right hand and they flew to Lilliana. Behind the queen was a creature with a bull's head and a man's body. He was doing awful things to the human souls lined up before him. It makes me sick to think about it. It was disturbing, something that men of the cloth like you two should never hear about. Honey and Regina joined up with Lilliana and they floated back to the tunnel of sparks. They burst out of there like an explosion from a champagne cork, landing far from Circle Seven and me. An evil soul had attached to them; I chased him down and returned him to his home. I looked back into the circle to see what happened to him but saw nothing. I am glad I cannot see everything down there. After the ordeal was over I heard them talking.

'I did have a joke to tell you down there,' said Honey. 'What is the definition of crazy?'

'I don't know,' said Regina.

'It is a witch flying through the fires of Hell and farting on her broomstick. That would singe your ass like your sister's eyelashes.'

Regina laughed so hard that she farted again. Khalen and Petal joined the three of them, not in farting but in laughing.

"I don't think they took Circle Seven seriously. What do you two think?" asked the knight.

"That was quite a tale," said Kirk Jr. "I never expected it to be funny."

"The only thing they seem to take seriously is taking our souls," said a more somber Kirk Sr. "Let's pray now, before you go."

During their prayer, strange music began in the garden below. Typically, fairies enjoy light music, peaceful and gentle sounds that make their heart happy. These were deep mysterious sounds, full of suspense and fear. The three of them found praying to be difficult. Gondemar, a devout monk, could not concentrate so he returned to his post. The ministers watched in wonder. Khalen had set a stage in the Fairy Garden for Lilliana and others to watch performances of Grimm's fairy tales.

To begin the first tale, an enormous wolf approached a beautiful little girl. The innocent child was not afraid (this was disturbing enough for the ministers), but then the little girl eagerly told the wolf where she was going and happily went on her way with no regard for danger. (The ministers shook their heads in disbelief.) The wolf made his way to the child's grandmother and devoured her. The little girl arrived moments later and the wolf consumed her alive as well. Finally, a woodsman came to the rescue. He cut open the wolf and saved the grandmother and the little girl.

The ministers were sickened, but heartened at Lilliana's reaction.

"This tale is awful," said the queen. "How will this help our cause?"

"What has happened in this tale is far worse than anything we have ever done to humans," explained Khalen. "Children will be thrilled when a powerful man makes the rescue. Although the man is not one of us, this will be known as a *fairy tale* because it has a happy ending. Fairy tales will always end well; children will love them and love us too. This is just a beginning. Let us have the next tale."

In the next show, the ministers watched as an evil stepmother displayed hatred toward her daughter, Snow White. The stepmother hated the girl because her beauty was far superior to the old hag. The evil stepmother ordered a man to take the girl to the woods and kill her. To prove that he killed her, the woodsman was required to bring back the heart, liver, and lungs for the stepmother to eat.

The man could not carry out the crime. He released the girl who found refuge with some friendly dwarves. The stepmother was outraged to find the girl was alive. Intent on harming the girl, she sent a poison apple that laid the girl in a coma. Finally, a prince rescued her and forced the stepmother to wear red-hot shoes and dance to her death.

"This is so gruesome," said Lilliana. "Dwarves have never been nice, but I do see your plan. Humans are much more violent than we could ever be. Everyone will like the romance and believe that even dwarves are loveable. When I think about how some humans are violent, I agree they deserve what happens to them in Circle Seven. Let us continue."

High up in the massive pine tree, Kirk Sr. shouted, "This will never work."

"Did you hear something, my king?" asked Lilliana.

"Perhaps the ministers are being entertained," said Khalen. "I hope they like fairy tales as much as you. I have one more."

In the final play, three stepsisters are jealous of Cinderella and mistreat her. They envy her small feet and try to wear her slippers. They get so frustrated that they cut off their own toes and heels to make the shoes fit. A fairy godmother grants the mistreated Cinderella a wish and she meets her prince. Birds peck out the eyes of the stepsisters and the mother for their wickedness. Cinderella finally finds happiness by having a wonderful relationship with her fairy godmother.

"I loved this story the best," said Lilliana. "The fairy godmother is wonderful; she holds our values for love and honor. Every girl will wish she had a fairy godmother and the boys will envy that. You are brilliant, my king."

At the end of the evening, the mood changed to a celebration. Khalen gave an announcement.

"These tales have been published today in our parallel world. From this time forward, people will love us. Our reputation will grow more and more positive with each passing year. We will soon become a small part of the human soul until the soul is our own. We have so much work to do, but it will be fun."

The ministers were stunned; silently they were praying when another knight appeared outside the tree.

"Ministers Kirk, I am the last Knight Templar to make your acquaintance. I am Nivard de Montdidier and I bring you good news along with my tale of Circle Eight."

"It's our pleasure to meet you Nivard," said Kirk Sr. "We've been witnessing a most troubling display of tales to be told to our children and grandchildren."

"We saw the plays too, and were repulsed," said Nivard. "I bring you good news about your book."

"What's the news?" asked Kirk Sr. eagerly.

"It's 1815 in the real world and your book has been published."

"That's wonderful news," said Kirk Jr. "I've had a change of heart and have been praying for that to happen. Real news about the fairies will counter these awful fairy tales."

"Sadly," countered Nivard, "the fairy tales began in 1812."

"It may be too late for my book to make a difference," added Kirk Sr. "My story may be looked upon as a fairy tale as well."

"We can only pray that your work is taken seriously," said Nivard.

"You are probably eager to tell us your tale," said Kirk Jr. "We've seen a lot today and need time to think about things."

"I understand," said Nivard. "If the fairy folk win out and take our souls, they will fill my Circle Eight. We will meet again at a better time. Congratulations for a published book. Your translation of the Bible was brilliant too. You really understood how fairies have interacted with man through the ages."

"Thank you, Nivard, for your kindness," said Kirk Sr. "Do you know how many translations of fairy tales have been made?"

"One-hundred and sixty translations in more than a hundred languages have been made," replied Nivard. "Don't despair. Someone will read your book."

"We will pray on it," said Kirk Sr. "We like your tales of fairies better and look forward to it."

CHAPTER 16

The Image Changes and the Battle Rages

For days on end, the final knight, Nivard de Montdidier, attempted to visit the ministers. Each day he found the tree bombarded with different shades of red electromagnetic waves. Montdidier had a wonderful reputation in key battles during the crusades; this enemy was like nothing he ever imagined. Day after day, he tried with all his might to penetrate the red cloak of energy. He became very concerned that he was taking a battering. For each shade of red, emotions ran through him deeply, emotions he had not felt since his formative years. The waves made him think deeply about negative, ugly thoughts and decisions he had made. At night, colors intensified, feelings of doubt and shame intensified until there was soothing, a calm reassurance that the fairies would take care of him. It was at this time he drew strength from his knighthood to weather the storm.

One particular night there was no moon, no clouds; the sky was black as pitch and curiously, there were no visible stars. A black crimson glow smothered the tree and emanated around Fairy Knowe. Khalen was in a dark mood; his favorite black stallion had died. He stood, defiant and angry, at the base of the tree.

"Ministers Kirk, end this ordeal now," demanded the king. "You have a hopeless struggle. Relinquish your free will; allow your souls to be free. We are a more deserving species. I have heard the knights telling you the tales about Hell. It exists in its current form because of the human race. You are a despicable species and undeserving of afterlife. Your children love my tales of violence; they love us as well. With each passing day, my stories are capturing their hearts and minds."

"My folk tale of Snow White will one day be shown on a large white wall in moving pictures (a powerful way to tell stories of violence and love for us). Many shows of fairy tales will follow. I will inspire a man to build a microcosm of our beautiful world, a magical kingdom."

"No one will believe this nonsense," stated Kirk.

"Your legend of finding fairies, Minister Kirk, is dead. Your family did not support you; humankind has abandoned you as a foolish eccentric found dead on a hill in your nightgown with your boots on. Give up your fight; make this easy for your son. The soul of man is crumbling within the human race. Many of your leaders will succumb to the demands of atheism and for the freedom to have no soul. Fair folk will thrive in the subconscious mind of man. Do you know what that means? Leaders in your world will do everything we tell them. They will work hard to eliminate religion. Your species is lost in the universe. Your fight is futile. End this ordeal now."

Nivard de Montdidier had heard enough. He called for a meeting of the Templars and they took action. Each proceeded to capture an evil soul headed to their respective circle. They escorted the spirits to Lilliana's palace garden where the spirits battled outside the Queen's bedroom.

The queen looked out her window and into the eyes of Nivard de Montdidier. He was holding two prisoners by the throat, men who committed terror in the name of God.

"Look and comprehend, Lilliana; see what your husband will become should he gain a soul. It is not God's will to impose your desires on the human race. These men deceived their own religion to build a legacy; Hell is their punishment. Khalen is deceiving God with his ambition. Your husband and King will burn in the black crimson light of Hell with these evil souls."

Lilliana screamed in horror; Khalen rushed to her side. To comfort his queen, he ceased bombarding the tree. The ordeal was over.

Nivard took the opportunity to visit the ministers. He could wait no longer to tell his tale. In terms of time in the natural world, two-hundred and fifty years had passed since the elder Kirk's capture.

"Are you well?" asked Nivard. "Do you want to hear my tale of Circle Eight?"

"I'm alert," said the father Kirk. "How are you doing son?"

No answer came from the younger Kirk.

"Is his soul still with you?" asked Nivard. "Can you tell whether or not he's still in this tree?"

"I hope he's just stunned," said the minister. "The red waves attacked us in many ways. They were subtle in the beginning, but soon challenged the core of our existence. Had Khalen taken possession of his soul, I am certain he would have boasted about his success. Tell me your tale. You have been doing your best to help us and we appreciate everything. A tale from Hell may help my son to come out of the darkness. It would be much better than the news Khalen constantly talks about. Is it true that fairy tales have captured the hearts and minds of people everywhere?"

"It is true good minister," said Nivard. "An attack on the human soul is coming from every direction. I am concerned that people will not understand the difference between themselves and beasts of the fields. There will be no strong souls like you to speak their minds and follow their hearts. My duties at Circle Eight are much greater than ever. I must tell my tale quickly for duties call."

"My son just mumbled something," said the minister. "He can hear you; please continue.

> *I was enjoying a light rain at Circle Eight when Petal Hailfrost and Honey Driftsfur, Khalen's royal guards, jogged into view from the main path. They were laughing, no doubt enjoying the rain as well from the look on their faces. I would love to feel the rain again. Petal wore green and violet to match her hair; Honey always wore gold to match her hair.*
>
> *'I will race you to the birdbath,' challenged Honey. 'Whoever wins gets to hold the baby owl.'*
>
> *The two beauties raced up the path. They got to the baby owl at the same time and began playing peekaboo with it. Khalen arrived on foot from the main path wearing a blue uniform for a change. Lilliana was by his side wearing a shiny white raincoat and a violet parasol. They joined Honey and Petal. Khalen gave the baby owl some chopped meat. He tossed a nice thick steak to the mother. She caught the meat with one claw, and then looked at me while she ate. I do miss eating steak.*
>
> *Suddenly a large black ball came rolling up the path heading directly to the birdbath. Petal and Honey stood prepared to protect the baby owl. Khalen drew his sword. A loud screeching sound came from the ball. The mother owl flew down and struck the ball; but it rolled on. Khalen stood ready to stick the ball with his sword, but with a pop, the ball burst; Sneaky McLittle, a leprechaun, stood before the group laughing hysterically.*
>
> *'Lollapalooza, I got you. I got all of you,' shouted Sneaky.*
>
> *'You little McSneakster,' said Petal. 'Come on Honey, we should tickle him to death.'*
>
> *The two fairies grabbed the leprechaun. Petal held him down and Honey tickled his feet until he cried, 'Lollapalooza!'*
>
> *'You are in much better spirits today,' said Khalen.*
>
> *'Am I better looking now?' asked Sneaky. 'Does my personality sparkle?'*
>
> *'Your personality is great; you are a charming McSneakster,' said Lilliana. 'I wish I could trust you.'*
>
> *'Sneaky, you've been chosen to go to Circle Eight for a reason,' said Khalen. 'Human folk that go there have used their personality to*

deceive others for their own benefit. They are guilty of the seven deadly sins.'

'We're all guilty of that in one way or another,' argued Sneaky. 'Look at the way we use humans. I just play the game better.'

'We do what we must for survival,' countered Khalen. 'You do it for profit, a major difference. Because you are good at it; you must pay attention to what you see down there.'

They walked up to me at Circle Eight, avoiding eye contact of course for they are uneasy around us. Khalen took Sneaky and Petal by the hand; they formed a circle, as was their pattern. They spun around seven times and together Lilliana and Honey shouted 'Reverse' sending them into a mist and into the pinhole of Circle Eight. I jumped to the hole as my counterparts instructed me and was able to see them; I was finally able to see what was down there.

They fell through a tunnel like heavy weights. Thin black lines against a light blue background got thicker and thicker until there were thin blue lines engulfed by total blackness. It was so black; I thought I had lost sight of them.

The sound of rock falling down the side of a mountain was all I could hear until a greenish light began to glow; it was coming from Petal's shoes. They were close to the edge of a cliff standing on a rock floor. Dark clouds appeared behind Sneaky; his left leg was dangling over the cliff. It was lucky for him that they were holding hands. More dark clouds were rising from below.

I heard Sneaky say, 'Something has a hold of my foot.'

A voice from below them said, 'I could be your best friend. You won't have to do anything. I'll take care of you. You deserve my protection. In return you just have to love me.'

'You make false promises,' shouted Petal.

She kicked the hand with her toe. The soul sighed and fell down the cliff, smacking into other souls making the climb.

'False promises are all these souls ever made,' explained Khalen. 'We are on a very narrow path. Petal, you must lead with Sneaky between us.'

'Sneaky, is there anything you want to say to me?' asked Petal.

'You said the right thing to that soul,' replied Sneaky, 'although we might need his protection.'

'Perhaps next time, I will let you go,' said Petal.

Sneaky shrugged his shoulders.

'Be kind to each other,' said Khalen. 'We have much to be concerned about. I do not know where the bottom is in this abyss.'

'I will radiate other light from my neon shoes,' offered Petal.

The greenish glow changed to violet, then pink, and then soft white.

'I still cannot see the bottom of the abyss,' said Khalen. 'I will place this gold coin on the path as a starting point; let us proceed. We can return here to navigate our way home.'

Petal's green shoes were glowing as she led them along a dark path around the mountain, constantly stepping on hands reaching over the edge of the cliff. I could hear a constant chatter from souls below them. They were arguing about their position and making promises to each other until there was a terrifying scream. Khalen stomped on two hands causing a soul to fall back into the void.

The fairies walked and walked until they came full circle. Ahead of Petal was the gold coin.

'I believe this circle empties into Circle Nine,' said Khalen. 'We can return home now. There are many cliffs down here but they are all the same.'

The three formed their circle on the tight ledge and ascended back to the tunnel where light blue stripes gradually turned into thin black stripes; they popped out of the tunnel and stood beside me.

I asked Khalen, 'Is this part of Hell as deep as I think it is?'

'Deeper,' was all Khalen said. Turning to Sneaky he said, 'I hope you have learned something from this experience. Take your knowledge to your people and tell them to be patient; mishandling a soul has terrible consequences.'

'I'll never end up down there, have a lollapalooza good day,' said Sneaky.

They hugged each other and went on their way. I looked back into the circle, but saw nothing. I wonder now about the faint screams I often hear. There is pain and fear from falling into the devil's den.

"No doubt," said Minister Kirk. "It's the devil's way of welcoming them."

"Hugues has seen the three-headed beast," said Nivard. "I won't spoil that tale for you. Did your son hear my tale?"

"Son," said the father, "can you hear us?"

Still there was no response from Kirk Jr.

"I'll return when he's feeling better and tell it again," said Nivard. All of us will pray for him, especially Rossal and Gondemar; they are very good at it. Peace be with you kind minister."

"Should fairies one day take possession of our soul, they would end up in your circle," stated the minister.

"I would send them all down there," said Nivard, "providing I'm still around. The danger is they know everything about us, what we think, feel, and need. They have already convinced their slaves that human folk are an inferior species, dependent on them for survival. Humans under their control know nothing about free will; their souls are so weak; it's pathetic I tell you."

"It's very sad," said the minister. "God can only help those who help themselves. Overall, your tale has lifted my spirit. Thank you."

CHAPTER 17

Khalen's Vision

I t was an inglorious and unusual spring morning. Dark clouds filled the sky; it was cold enough to snow. Minister Kirk was still without the companionship of his son, the younger Kirk still locked into a period of darkness and solitude, with only an occasional mumble. From atop the pine tree the minister watched as King Khalen and Queen Lilliana led a small brigade down the main path on horseback. It started snowing; there was a flash of lightning and a crack of thunder.

"This is an amazing morning to have the Crocus Festival," said Lilliana.

"Mother nature has brought us an unexpected gift of power, excitement, and beauty," commented Khalen. "An electrical charge has been generated to bring new life; the first flower of spring will bloom today."

"It is symbolic, very much like what you are doing for us," said Lilliana. "The crocus refreshes the planet. I can only imagine how this celebration will feel when I have a soul."

They rode to a wild garden on the eastern side of the hill. It began snowing; the once bare garden had signs of new growth, its green leaves nearly covered with snow. The fairies formed a circle around the garden with great anticipation. Khalen was the first to dismount his young black stallion; the rest followed him. Musicians began to play soft, elegant sounds while dancers, dressed in purple and white, glided around the garden in a fluid motion. Another crack of thunder filled the air. Khalen raised his arms; the dancers and musicians stopped. The King walked to the edge of the garden at its northernmost point. Everyone circled the nearly snow-covered garden.

Lilliana extended her arm to her husband, as was their tradition; all were about to join hands when unexpectedly, Khalen went into a trance. Lilliana looked upon him with concern, knowing immediately that he was having a vision. This was very rare, somewhat exciting, yet also dangerous. The silence of winter covered the field as they held hands and collectively held their breath, with the exception of Khalen.

Khalen was fixated. In his mind, he travelled back to the circle garden under the minister's pine. He focused on the mother owl staring intently into a mist of fog forming just outside the garden. An intruder suddenly appeared out of the mist surrounded by knights, the ones who guarded the nine circles to Hell. The intruder stepped toward him. Feeling threatened as if the images were real, Khalen drew his sword frantically and stepped into the crocus garden. Without any awareness, he had slashed Lililiana's dress. She screamed.

Still fixated in his vision, he believed Lilliana's scream was her fear of the attackers. He shouted, "Enter my garden at the risk of losing your life. I will have room for you in my tree. The minister's souls are soon to be mine."

The intruder responded, "The soul of man will endure! I am Bobby Kirk, the seventh great grandson of Robert E. Kirk. Like my ancestral grandfather, I have the gift of second sight. I have come to free him. You need to fear me for your life. Release him or prepare to die!" The image of the younger Kirk held his right fist forward; and with his left hand, he clutched at his chest.

Holding his sword forward, Khalen took another step, staggered and fell into the crocus garden crushing many of the white and purple crocuses blooming in the snow. His trance was broken; his vision had ended.

"Khalen, my love," screamed Lilliana, "What just happened?"

There was another crack of thunder. The mother owl from high atop Fairy Knowe swooped down from the minister's tree and landed in the garden, destroying many more of the delicate flowers.

Lilliana knelt beside Khalen. He looked at the slash in her dress and then his sword he had dropped on the flowers. "What have I done? Are you injured?"

"It is only my dress," said Lilliana. "You had a vision; what did you see?"

"I am so sorry," said Khalen. "I have ruined our celebration. This was a powerful vision. An ancestor of our captive ministers is coming to challenge me. The Knights Templar stood behind him in formation. The invader confronted me to engage in battle. He wants the minister released."

"How do you know that he is an ancestor," asked Lilliana.

"His name is Bobby Kirk," said Khalen. "He told me that he has the gift of second sight like the elder Kirk." Khalen rose to his feet and helped Lilliana to hers.

"I have had a vision and have seen an invader," announced the king. "He challenged me here at Fairy Knowe. We will find this Bobby Kirk. He will join his ancestors in the minister's tree. Our festival must end now. We have much work to do. Once we possess the human soul, I will receive prophecies in dreams while safely lying in my bed. I apologize deeply for startling everyone. The beauty of the crocus and the rebirth of spring have combined to bring us this warning. We will prevail."

There was another streak of lightning and crack of thunder. It started raining; the snow became muddy; the crocuses closed their petals for their roots to have a drink.

Minister Kirk watched the fairies trudge back to the palace. His spirit soared with hope and joy. Moments later, Hugues de Payens paid him a visit.

"Did you hear the great news?" asked the knight. "Help is on the way."

"Thank God," said the minister. "I saw what happened, but I don't understand."

"Fair folk don't dream," explained the grand master. "You need a soul to dream. Fair folk have pleasant thoughts when they are sleeping, but they cannot do any soul travelling to connect with a loved one. They have visions where they see the future. It is similar to what prophets do, only more powerful. Typically, they foresee death and destruction. Their accuracy is complete. What Khalen saw will come true. The question is when will it happen? We can rejoice in this news."

"My joy is tempered; my son is still not responding," said Kirk.

"I heard the news, father," said the son rather weakly. "I've been trying to communicate with you; I've been in a shell."

"What a wondrous day," said the elder Kirk. "I'm so happy to hear you, my son. My seventh great grandson is coming. The fairy folk had their celebration; we're having ours."

"Khalen has had everything going his way until this news," said Hugues. "Our world has become infatuated with fairies. Khalen has seduced the thoughts of leaders; the world needs a true leader. The progress humanity has made since the time of Christ is in decline. Man's soul has become weakened."

"I heard Khalen say he only wanted to transplant strong souls," said the younger Kirk.

"He wants the first transplants to be strong," said the knight. "After he's successful with his transplant, he believes any good soul will meet his needs, for the soul can be strengthened. He hopes the final conquering will be when humans voluntarily give up their souls. He never considered the possibility of an adversary."

"Is there anything to be done to help our great grandson?" asked the younger Kirk.

"Pray my dear ministers," said the knight. "We must all try to communicate with him through prayer. Khalen has no concept of prayer; he can't defeat something he doesn't understand. He knows about its energy, and is eager to learn about prayers and dreaming, but he knows nothing. Pray with deep, vivid meditation. My Knights Templar will do the same."

"How many years have passed since my death?" asked the elder Kirk.

"It's been three-hundred and fifty years," replied Hugues. "It's God's will. You had the gift as a seventh son and now your seventh great grandson follows you. That is wonderful news. Give praise to God."

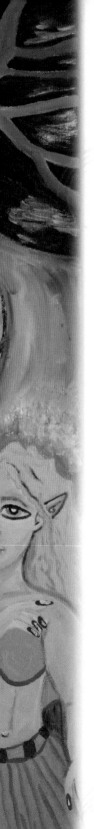

CHAPTER 18

❦

Connecting Through Dreams

Bobby Kirk had just completed his exams for his junior year at college after studying nearly the whole night. He returned to his room and his bed where he desperately needed some rest. After only a few moments, he began to dream:

In a thick fog, there are strange voices, child-like voices for adults. Colorful shapes begin to emerge through a fog. I am here on a mission and I feel like nothing can stop me. A massive pine tree in front of me takes shape, as the fog becomes a mist. A thick grassy circle divided by a wavy, white stone path and bordered with flower gardens comes clearly into view. It is the most beautiful garden I have ever seen. Colorful ground lighting underneath mushrooms of varied sizes and colors are around the perimeter. Fragrant rose-scented candles light the white wavy stone path through the garden and circle the pine tree. Soft white light, like moon glow through a mist, fills the space. It provides a rich, almost liquid aspect to the colors. Blossoming roses above the mushrooms add to the scent of the candles.

I have been here many times to feel the joy and beauty of this place. The child-like voices become louder and fairy folk begin to appear. The garden becomes full of them; they are having a party. My heart is pounding in my chest.

On a low branch of the pine tree, a white owl lifts her wings. She has a small sharp black beak, her bright yellow eyes staring at me. Standing near the main path, just outside the circle and next to her stallion, is the fairy queen, Lilliana. She is wearing a crown of starflowers with baby's breath, and a white wrist orchid. Holding the leather rein to her white stallion, she faces her steed to adjust a ring of the same type of flowers. As she turns to walk across the wavy stone path, her blue satin dress sparkles. Stopping at a landscaped birdbath, she pets a baby owl perching on a tiny bridge. The queen raises her right arm to show off her wrist orchid, and cups her hand to receive the mother owl gliding down from her lookout perch. This startles a small spotted rabbit to dart through the crowd and jump into the lap of a beautiful young woman; she's unmistakably human and very interesting.

The mother owl continues to stare at me even as the queen places the bird next to the baby owl. The mother owl touches the baby's beak and quickly looks back at me. The queen takes her seat in the circle near the massive pine tree. The mother owl glides back to her lookout position; she continues to stare at me.

To the left side of the tree a group of musicians begins to play their instruments. They play a tune that's upbeat and clear. A group of bare-

foot dancers, dressed in colors of the rainbow, enters the circle. They began by leaping in the air like ballet dancers. Circling around the tree, they dance for their queen.

The beautiful young woman smiles, a worrisome, compassionate smile, not like the sad smiles of the others.

King Khalen arrives on a black stallion, dismounts, and the dancing stops. He crosses the stone path to stand next to his queen. Behind his chair is a black box with levers. Looking all around, he notices the white owl staring at me. Khalen studies the owl and then looks at me.

I become visible to everyone.

The king draws his sword accidentally slashing Lilliana's gown. With his other hand, he reaches for a lever on the black box by his chair and gives it a pull. A dense red light permeates the circle and there is total silence. The king points his sword and everyone looks at me. The joy in their eyes has turned to fear.

I am ready for battle. Standing behind me in a three by three formation are the Knights Templar, swords vertical with handles at their chests. The mother owl swoops down from the tree to attack me; the knights raise their swords in my defense sending the owl upward to avoid the blades. Lilliana's stallion rears her front legs; on the horse's back is a beautiful young fairy sitting proudly in the saddle. She is somehow on my side. My heart is pounding even more; I feel a warm sensation and clutch at an object on my chest.

"Enter my garden at the risk of losing your life," shouts Khalen. I have room for you in my tree. The ministers' souls are soon to be mine." He waves his sword.

"I am Bobby Kirk. *The soul of man will endure!*" shouted Bobby coming out from deep within his dream. Holding his right fist forward, he sat up in bed ready to fight just as his roommate came into the dorm room.

"I know who you are," said his roommate, Colin. "Did you sell your soul for a good grade or what? You're sweating."

"That was nuts," said Bobby. "These dreams are going to drive me insane. I've got to do something."

"What happened? That sounded more like a nightmare."

"Forget about it, man," said Bobby. "It was nothing."

"I know you too well, buddy. What are you talking about?" continued Colin. "What the hell happened?"

"I've had some recurring dreams; they're getting more intense, more frequent, and a bit too real. I've got to do something about them."

"I studied recurring dreams in psychology this past semester; they are important for threat avoidance. Dreams offer important information to protect you in a survival situation. How many recurring dreams have you had?"

"You won't believe this. I have had sixteen dreams total. This is the seventh time I have had this one dream, only this time it continued. It really rocked me."

"Sixteen dreams, are you serious? Are they related? What do you dream about?"

"I'm dead serious; I wrote them down. It feels odd talking about this," said Bobby. "You're probably thinking I'm nuts."

"I already know you're a nut case, Bobby. That is why we are friends. You can talk to me about anything. This is obviously bothering you. Tell me what's going on."

"The dreams are definitely related and they seem so real. It is hard to explain. They're nothing like regular dreams."

"You look rocked, Bobby. Listen, dreams can help you solve problems while you are sleeping. As crazy as they seem, there could be an answer somewhere in the chaos. Dreams that seem real carry much more meaning. What happened?"

"You couldn't possibly understand," explained Bobby. "I'm like transported to another place and time, actually another world. I must find a way to make them stop. They're going to push me over the edge."

"Tell me about them. You know I research everything. Dreams are fascinating. Our subconscious mind works overtime to solve problems. Tell me as much as you remember. Let me read what you have written; I will study them. Bizarre dreams are the best."

"I don't know about showing you my journal. I would be so embarrassed if you ever told anyone about it."

"I'd never do anything to embarrass you. It sounds like you need some help with this. Two heads are better than one, and this stuff is right up my alley. I've been studying these things."

"If I show the journal to you, will you promise me that you'll not tell anyone?"

"I said I'd never embarrass you and I meant it," said Colin. "I understand your privacy about a journal. Tell me about the dreams and you may get some relief from talking about them. There's no dream that can make you look crazy. In fact, I think the opposite's true. Wilder dreams mean you're more creative and that's just intelligence. Let me be your therapist. I'll take notes and this'll be a good experience for me when I start my practice. If that doesn't happen, I may need a shrink one day and I'll know how to pick a good one."

"You'll need one after you hear all this," said Bobby.

"What are friends for?"

"You asked for it," said Bobby. "Perhaps you should make an appointment with the school psychologist before we start. In all my dreams, I've been an invisible visitor to another world. As I said, this was the seventh time I've had this particular dream. For the first time, there was a change; I was visible to them, the fair folk or good folk as they call themselves. I looked into the eyes of an enemy. I had to fight their leader."

"By calling them fair folk, are you talking about fairies?"

"I know it sounds weird, but these dreams are real. These beings called fairies look very much like us. Calling them fairies makes the circumstances seem silly like when you were a kid and had your tooth pulled, or talk about little girl's fairy godmother, dumb stuff like that. In my dreams, they're just as real as we are. Don't think about fairies like in fairy tales. They're kind of like aliens except they call themselves fair folk and look very much like humans. I see my seventh great grandfather in the dreams and he calls them fairies. In his time, (I researched this) people were afraid of fairies. They are far from harmless."

"It's got to be the stress of finals," offered Colin. "You've had a tough junior year." Placing his hand on his friend's shoulder he said, "What you need is to get to the ocean, drink a couple of brews, and date some girls. That'll be fifty dollars unless you have more to tell."

"I knew you'd think I was nuts. I have had these dreams since I was twelve years old. This has nothing to do with my junior year or final exams."

"I was just trying to be funny with the money. I don't think you're nuts. I have heard about fair folk mythology. It is somewhat hard to wrap my head around fairies being real. I can grasp the idea of aliens much better; perhaps you're having something like an alien abduction."

"Call them what you like," said Bobby. "They look just like us. In my sixteen dreams, they are fairies, fairy folk, or good folk. I see them very clearly; more than dreams, they are like out of body experiences. What's your rate for that?"

"For out-of-body experiences, OBEs in professional terms, I charge much more," said Colin. "But seriously, OBE is the soul detaching itself from the body and travelling in space. Some people believe it's drug-induced; a real OBE is different. Most people report some kind of spirit walking or soul travelling. I have never done it, but I have read that one out of every ten people report similar experiences. What's it like?"

"I see and hear things very clearly. Before the dream I just had, I was invisible to just about everything except an owl. I cannot explain this, but somehow the dreams came to me from my seventh great grandfather. Just now, I looked into the eyes of an enemy and was about to fight him. I also became visible to knights guarding the gates of Hell (nine other worlds parallel to theirs and ours). Fairies have the ability to become astral beings and can easily travel from their world to ours. The knights in my dreams have seen the fairies pass through the gateways into Hell and return. I have seen it all in my dreams. It's like I was there."

"Let me pick my jaw up off the floor. Now that's amazing," said Colin; he paused to think about it. "I'd like to see what you've seen. Can I read your journal? Who is your ancestral great grandfather? Was he a war hero?"

"From my dreams, I know he's my seventh great grandfather; I call him Gramps. He was a minister to a church in Aberfoyle, Scotland and wrote two books. He made a translation of the Bible, and he wrote a book about the lives of subterranean inhabitants, elves, fauns, and fairies from his daily studies of their behavior."

"Didn't people think he was mentally challenged?" asked Colin.

"Fairies were very real to people back then. No one questioned their existence. They were a serious threat with baby abductions, stealing grain, and anything else. Everyone respected my grandfather and never questioned his findings. People were afraid of fairies and not only in Scotland. There were even reports from North America about fairies being different from their European counterparts. People back then were afraid my grandfather was making fairies angry by studying them so closely. They never doubted for a moment that his findings were real."

"Didn't he have to prove what he was seeing?"

"He did that. Doppelgangers are fairies that attach themselves to humans. When a person is about to die, the doppelganger leaves the body. Gramps saw what was happening and as their minister he was able to intervene or predict a death."

"How do you know this?"

"I've read all about him. He had a master's degree, translated the Bible, and was a very good minister. He understood the history of fairy folk. No one doubted what he saw. While he was writing his book on subterranean inhabitants, he died on Doon Hill, also known as Fairy Knowe in the parallel world. People back then say that he learned too much about the fairies and they took his life. History states the fairies took his soul and locked him in a massive pine tree. It is a legend, of course, but back then, it was real to everyone who knew him. I know he is communicating with me in these dreams."

"Wow, that's intense," said Colin. "How are you certain he's communicating with you?"

"I just know it; I feel a connection to him. We have some things in common," explained Bobby.

"The mind is a very powerful thing, and things can seem very real," said Colin not convinced.

"There's something else we have in common, a major similarity," said Bobby. "Let me close the window, and check the hallway before I tell you."

Bobby closed the window, checked all around the room, and hallway. He sat down at Colin's desk and Colin sat on his bed.

"I have never told anyone this before," said Bobby. "In a dream Gramps told me to never to let fairies know that I have the gift of second sight, and to look through them as if they weren't there. I have always followed his advice. Whenever one of them looks at me, I relax and look through them."

Colin said nothing.

"Are you thinking I'm mentally challenged?" asked Bobby.

"I've got a million issues going through my head;" said Colin, "none of which are about you being mentally challenged. At death, there's a loss of weight and an electrical charge and there's the first law of thermodynamics where energy can't be created or destroyed."

"We have to get moving. Let's talk more on the way to the beach," said Bobby. "It's a relief for me to finally tell someone about this. I have a journal with all my real dreams as I call them. You can read the journal, but I have to caution you to be careful with what you say. Based on my dreams, we could be in danger if they discover who I am. There are so many fairy spirits in our world. They look just like us or they can change size. I can see them easily, so I know when it's safe to talk."

"It's hard to grasp why they would find you a threat," posed Colin.

"Capturing my grandfather's soul was just the beginning for the fairies. They want to steal the human soul and make it part of their own DNA. Fairy folk are centuries older than us and more evolved; the soul is the only difference between our species. The Fairy King believes I'm coming to fight him for my grandfather's release; he also believes that with this battle he could lose the opportunity for eternal life not just for himself but for his people."

"I see," said Colin looking somewhat unconvinced.

"Everyone in Scotland knows the legend about my grandfather's soul being locked inside the Fairy Tree," continued Bobby. "Many people have claimed they have looked into the parallel world of Fairy Knowe, a parallel space that exists alongside Doon Hill. No one knows about the connections to the nine other parallel worlds that we call Hell. Call it a legend or call it history, but it is well known that fairies have always wanted man's soul. I believe they are close to making my grandfathers' soul their own and he is reaching out to me. They also captured my grandfather's son Robert E Kirk Jr. In my dreams, I must fight for their release. The mortal fear for fairies is that humans will invade their world with iron weapons before they have gained possession of our soul. I would be the biggest threat to them and their goal of having eternal life."

"I've heard about some of the legends," said Colin. "It's true; many people still believe they exist, and are still causing problems. Listen Bobby, reoccurring dreams are very important and need exploration. As I said, your subconscious mind is trying to resolve a problem. It is working overtime to get you to do something. You have changed your major now three times, and you are still not happy with your future. Perhaps these dreams are caused by that?"

"These dreams have been occurring and recurring for years. I'm serious about needing to do something."

"You should do something. When can I read your journal?"

"I'll read it to you while you're driving us to the beach," said Bobby. "Keep an open mind and don't tell anyone about this."

"I take all science seriously," said Colin. "I always have an open mind. Everything you are saying makes sense; I need to study it. The multiverse theory claims there are three different types of parallel worlds, and most likely eleven dimensions exist on our planet. String theory also supports this. These are different time/space dimensions created during the big bang and exist millimeters away from us, like a stack of paper. These spaces are growing."

"That explains more than you know," said Bobby.

"I admire your ancestral grandfather," continued Colin. "It sounds like he had great self-confidence, and he explored things with a scientific approach. I love that about him. I'm not very much into religion, although I believe in God. I also believe Jesus planted the seeds of democracy. Two-thousand years later the world is a much better place because of him. Your great grandfather was probably one of very few men in his time to have both a strong religious foundation and a strong academic background.

"Every day he studied these beings just like we do in science labs. At the time, no one thought he was strange."

"We need to explore these dreams in a scientific manner just like your ancestor explored the unknowns in his life."

"Thanks for being my friend," said Bobby, sounding relieved. "I've decided what I must do. I'm going to Scotland for the summer. Perhaps after you read my journal you'll understand me."

"Wow that was unexpected," said Colin. "What about the girls we met last weekend? You will miss a lot of fun. You will also lose your lifeguard job and a lot of money from not working this summer. Money will be scarce for your senior year."

"I'll miss all of it. I have to go soon, tomorrow if possible. I cannot explain it; but I must get some answers. I do not want these dreams to drive me over the edge of sanity. Have you ever heard of the gift of second sight?"

"Yea, I saw it happen Saturday night when you gave those freshmen girls a double take. That worked out well. We have dates this weekend."

"I'm not talking about a second look. Anyway, you can still meet them," said Bobby. "There are other lifeguards at the beach house. You won't have any problem finding a volunteer to go with you."

"It wouldn't be the same," said Colin. "I get tongue tied around girls. I would be more confident with you there. The short blonde babe gave you a kiss; that is what I call a double take. Can't you plan your trip next week?"

"I'll see what I can do, but you may have to meet them without me. I've got a lot to do and a lot to think about." Bobby opened his journal.

"This is serious," said Colin. "I can't be a lone knight on Saturday. Perhaps I can help you. A trip to Scotland sounds like a great adventure. I will make a deal with you. Keep the date for Saturday night and I'll go to Scotland with you."

"You need to think about that," said Bobby. "Read my journal first, and I'm sure you'll rethink that offer. I am meeting my grandparents for lunch today. After that, we can head for the beach. I will make plans to travel next Monday. A few days won't make a big difference."

"Thanks buddy," said Colin. "I'm serious about going to Scotland. My parents planned my life; I want to have an adventure, something unplanned and extraordinary. As I see it, we go to Scotland, figure out what is causing these dreams, date a few Scottish lasses, and then come home. What could be better than that? You could introduce me to a couple of fairy chicks. I understand they're very sexy."

"They would make you a slave," said Bobby.

"Is there a problem with that?" asked Colin.

"Be packed and ready to drive after lunch," said Bobby. "Don't stop to talk to the beauty with green hair and champagne eyes standing on your left shoulder."

"I'm definitely going to Scotland now," said Colin. "I'll be ready to go. What is another student loan going to do to me? I'll be poor but have great memories. Did you just see something with that gift of second sight?"

"You will not believe what I have to tell you on the car ride."

Bobby visited his grandparents for lunch, called his parents, and was able to get all the information he needed for his trip. When he returned he found Colin packed and ready to go.

"My family is fully behind me taking this trip," said Bobby. My grandparents are going to send me some money. They also said they have an old relic they are sending me. It's from Scotland and has been in the family for years; it dates back to the time of my Gramps."

"Did you tell them the whole story?" asked Colin.

"I told them the trip may be for only two weeks, but I wanted to explore this part of my family history while I was young.

My father said he travelled through Europe when he was in college and asked whether you were going too. I told him that you were thinking about it."

"I am going," said Colin. "We made a deal for Saturday night, and I've concluded that you may need some help over there. Between the Scottish lasses and cute fairies, you would have so many stories; I would regret not going for the rest of my life. I can't let that happen."

"We can travel on Monday," said Bobby. "I've got all the details. Let's head to the beach."

"Do you have your journal handy? I want to hear some of it."

"All I ask is that you keep your eyes on the road," said Bobby. "Pull over if at any time you need to."

They headed down the road. Bobby explained he had had dreams about all nine circles of Hell, dreams about his grandfathers, and dreams about different things in the fairy realm such as baby abductions and battles.

Colin was most interested in the confrontation with the fairy king. Bobby read that dream to him and the addendum he had added today where he became visible to everyone. Once Colin had heard that story, he wanted to know about the journeys to Hell. Bobby explained again the dreams were so real and decided to read about the discovery of Hell; it started with the ninth circle and the grandmaster of the Knights Templar, Hugues de Payens. The journal read as follows:

Real Dream #6 Discovery of Hell – Circle Nine

I am sitting behind Queen Lilliana on her white stallion. With no idea that I am there, she surveys the battlefield before her. Human ghosts are tormenting fairies running in every direction. Suddenly a fireball darts from the field, flies past us and up the path of the hill. Lilliana gives the stallion a kick and we chase the fireball. A knight (that is the spirit of a knight) snatched the fiery orb out of the air. The fiery orb turned into a human ghost; the knight held the tormented spirit by the scruff of his neck. Lilliana charged on.

'Wait there,' she shouted to the knight, her horse galloping even faster.

The ghostly apparition of the knight did not wait; he hurled the burning ghost into a hole. Lilliana pulled the stallion to a stop and dismounted; I floated along with her as she knelt down to look in the hole.

'What did you do?' demanded Lilliana.

'I am Hugues de Payens, grand master of the Knights Templar,' said the knight. 'The evil one you pursue has gotten to where he needed to go. If you had business with him, it is too late. He's in Hell now.'

'What is your business here?' questioned Lilliana. 'I wanted to see this fiery orb. What did you do to him?'

'This is the Ninth circle of Hell,' explained the knight. 'I assist evil souls to enter here; none of them goes willingly. I also protect the earth from evil trying to escape from here; none has ever escaped. My fellow knights guard the other eight circles. We do this for the good of humankind. Since you have no soul, this should not concern you. Should you have any interest in going down there, be wary. This is the devil's domain.'

As in my other dreams, the knight had no idea I was with them. I looked into the hole with Lilliana. It was deep; the fiery orb was descending toward an abyss of fire. There was heat coming from the hole and a strong smell of sulfur, the foulest scent imaginable.

'Have you or your knights been down there?' asked Lilliana.

'No, these circles are for evil souls, souls small enough to enter. Strong souls are too big to fall through the holes. We can no longer see and hear anything down there. The space has grown dense and foul. Those who betray the trust of others go to this circle. This is the deepest part of Hell for the most evil.'

'Is this position your punishment?' questioned Lilliana.

'This mission is our honor,' replied Hugues. 'We will bypass the outer universe and enter Heaven when our mission is complete. We protect the universe from evil. It is an honor for us to be protectors. Our time will come when we will bask in the eternal light. The sun will ultimately consume Earth, with all its realms. Like you, our work will end on this planet. Unlike you, I will go on. I know you seek to steal the soul of man; you would find a home in Hell should you succeed in your effort.'

Lilliana shrugged her shoulders, 'I am going down there.'

I stood behind her with my hands on her shoulders; we spun like a top and like a vapor, we entered the small pinhole, a tunnel of darkness. The air felt thick; the sulfur smell intensified with rotten eggs. I somehow was able to hold my breath. Pitch-black darkness became a deep red.

Suddenly we popped out of the tunnel into open space. A trace of the lightning bolt below us was piercing deep into the chasm. Like a magnet, something pulled us toward a frozen lake, a frozen lake on fire. It was a world of fire and ice. Lilliana attempted to change our direction; she struggled to go left then right; either gravity or some other force was pulling us down.

As we got closer and closer to the lake of fire and ice, I heard screams, moans, and crying. Human ghosts were buried in the ice, some deeper than others, yet they were on fire.

Suddenly another fireball shot past us and penetrated the lake. The shape of a man emerged; demonic looking creatures swarmed around him until the man burst into flames. The ice changed from bright white to deep blue and then to blood red. A creature with three heads of these colors emerged before us; I was looking directly in the faces of the devil, frozen in ice up to his waist.

To the left was his blue face, not a pretty blue but a dirty blue because of a lack of blood flow; his tears were frozen on his pocked marked face. On the right side, I looked at his white face, pale and pocked marked with foam at the mouth. The reddish face in the center had boils with steam oozing from them. His yellowish, jaundiced eyes reflected the fire in the ice; this face was laughing. Lilliana turned her head; she was sickened and horrified.

'*I've never had a visitor like you before,*' *said the white face.* '*Who have you betrayed?*' *asked the blue one.* '*What do you want?*' *asked the red face followed by a chilling laugh.*

'*I will leave now,*' *said Lilliana.* '*I apologize for my intrusion.*'

The devil laughed; his laughter grew louder and louder as we float-ed back to the dense red tunnel that carried us back to the pinhole at Fairy Knowe. We emerged through the hole to stand beside the knight. He drew his sword. I let go of Lilliana's shoulders.

'*I saw and heard everything and smelled the rotten eggs,*' *said Hu-gues.* '*You survived it. I admire your bravery. There must be some good in you.*'

The knight paused for a moment and added, '*However, I must give you a warning. I know you have the soul of Reverend Kirk. You need to release him. Should you steal the human soul, your fate will reside somewhere in one of these circles. You use humans for your own desires. That kind behavior will find you permanent residence in that icy lake of fire. Thank you for lighting up the circle and showing the devil to me again.*'

'*I never want to see that beast again,*' *said Lilliana.* '*Have things changed dramatically down there?*'

'*Hell has become darker over the centuries. The light around you made everything visible, to me,*' *said the knight.* '*Centuries ago light filtered down from the sun. I shared what I knew with the poet, Dante Alighieri. He made good use of the information in a poem. I suggest you read it. Since that time, Hell has become too dark and too dense for us to see down there. From what I have seen today, this circle of Hell has become larger and fouler. The devil remains the same.*'

'*I commend you on having a poet deliver your message,*' *said Lil-liana.* '*I must tell this to Khalen. You must show me the other eight circles. Your knights can see things first hand. We have something in common, dear knight. We are the first to witness the devil's domain.*'

"You called me dear," *said Hugues.* "Are you not repulsed in seeing me?"

'*You are unnerving to say the least,*' *said Lilliana.* '*I can bare-ly contain my happiness with this discovery. My husband and I want strong souls. We will possess a soul one day, and we will make far better use of it than your species ever could. We will learn a lot from this discovery. Show me the other circles; your knights will learn from what we discover.'*

'I will show you each circle and you will meet the knights who guard them. You need to know what will happen to good folk should you succeed in your quest. Your visit has restored my energy, and the belief in my mission,' concluded Hugues de Payens.

The other knights joined us at Circle Nine; everything faded away.

"I never thought about Hell as a physical place," said Colin. "Space and time are relative within dimensions with no relationship to one an-other. You saw the devil in a dream. How do you feel about that?"

"All the time I was there, I felt protected," said Bobby. "I've seen the worst and I believe I can face anything. I don't plan to see him again."

"So you went to the other eight circles?"

"I did. There were different fairies and a different knight at each cir-cle. You will definitely think I am nuts after these journeys. I went to each world, but I always knew Gramps was somehow showing me what he had seen. I never once thought I could be trapped there."

"I had nightmares after my first funhouse," said Colin. "Your Gramps is preparing you for anything and everything."

"I can only imagine how strong he must be," added Bobby. "Are you sure you want me to read this to you? Will you get nightmares?"

"There's a scientific reason for everything," said Colin. "I try to look at things from that point of view; I'll be fine. I was hoping you had some beautiful fairies to tell me about."

"I've seen some who could cloud your thinking," said Bobby.

"Well," said Colin, "if I have to go through Hell first before I see them, then let's do it."

They laughed and then Bobby proceeded to read the other eight jour-neys to Hell, giving additional information where Colin was interested. Colin especially liked Honey Driftsfur and Petal Hailfrost; they were very cute. By the time they reached the lifeguard's beach house, they finalized their plans to travel to Aberfoyle, Scotland, on Monday. Within minutes after arriving, they arranged a minimum two-week stay with a flexible re-turn flight home. Both agreed they hoped to resolve Bobby's issues quickly and return home to their summer jobs, although Colin was prepared to spend the entire summer if necessary.

For the first time in his life, Bobby had shared his secret world. He was so grateful he had a friend with an open mind, and a friend who could help him explore what was happening to him. He warned Colin several times about the danger of talking openly about their situation. He also made him promise to keep his gift of second sight a secret; it was his only weapon against this enemy.

CHAPTER 19

SECRETS REVEALED

fter having some pizza and settling into the beach house, Colin wanted to know more. Bobby had already sighted a large number of fairies looking for some summer vacation action. He suggested they talk on the beach out in the open to ensure privacy. They needed to avoid the boardwalk and amusement park; there were many cozy corners and prime locations where fairies did their work.

They walked to a secluded spot on the shore far from the boardwalk. "This is a good location," said Bobby. I can see in all directions."

"So, what can you tell me about these sightings?" questioned Colin. "How long have you had the gift and what do you see?"

"I've had it my whole life," said Bobby. "When I was very young, my Gramps visited me in a dream. He told me not to be afraid of them, never make eye contact, and look right through them as if they were not there. I watch and study them in a passive way. He told me I would know what to do when the time comes. I've always followed his advice."

"You are a strong person," said Colin. "I would've lost my nerve a long time ago and told somebody. Have you ever seen any of them when I was with you?"

"Fairies love weddings," said Bobby. "They really put on a show mocking everything that goes on. They were at my sister's beach wedding."

"Wow," said Colin. "That was quite a wedding. You set off fireworks early to surprise your sister."

161

"I set off the fireworks for a good reason," explained Bobby. "I watched as fairies assembled above a low cloud at the edge of the ocean just behind the ceremony. They had copied every detail to mock my sister. Their bridesmaids wore pink and carried the same flowers. It looked like they had raided the kitchen for food and were eating during their ceremony. Fairy doubles were there; they looked just like my sister and her fiancé. I got so angry; I sent a cannonball into the middle of the cloud underneath them. The explosion rocked them and they spilled their drinks."

"I remember the explosion; you sent a red dragon to follow the cannonball," added Colin.

"The timing was perfect," said Bobby. "Right after the explosion, the red streak went through the group and out to sea. They watched it form into a dragon and make a U-turn; and then I launched the phoenix. The dragon returned to meet the phoenix on their cloud. The fairies looked like deer in headlights. I wanted to tell you why I was laughing so hard but I had to keep it a secret."

"The fireworks were great and your sister was so happy. You told everyone the marriage of the phoenix and the dragon was the symbol of a harmonious marriage."

"That's the legend, but it wrecked the marriage of the good folk."

"What else have you seen?" asked Colin.

"I once had a robbery happen in front of me. It was two years ago when I was a clerk at the meat market."

"What happened?"

"An elderly lady was paying me for her purchase when I saw a fairy stalking her. He stood about three steps behind her and stared at her purse. She looked nervous although she had no idea he was there. I kept an eye on him; I looked through him as if he was not there, never making eye contact. With total focus on his victim, he was quick as a cat and stole a twenty-dollar bill out of her purse. She was stunned at having no money, certain that it was there before she came in the store."

"What did you do?" asked Colin.

"I hit a switch locking the front door; it trapped the fairy. The woman looked frightened; I told her to be patient, that perhaps she dropped her money and that I would check the store. I was so angry; I broke my rule of not making eye contact and walked directly at him.

The fairy looked confused and panicked. He ran to the walk-in refrigerator and went inside. I followed him in there and picked up a meat cleaver from the butcher's block. He sat in the corner to wait me out.

Holding my meat cleaver as a weapon, I inched closer and closer to him. He dropped the twenty-dollar bill; I bent over to pick it up, and he rushed past me and out of the refrigerator. I returned the money to the elderly lady and unlocked the front door. The fairy rushed past me to get outside."

"What did you say to her?"

"I told her she must have dropped the money when selecting her purchase. She looked confused but was happy with that; I never saw that fairy again."

"That was intense. Could the fairy have hurt you?"

"I don't think so. All I thought about was the thief stealing from the poor old lady. They will steal anything they can, and for no reason. The eye contact made him very uncomfortable. I was ready to swing the cleaver. It scared me later to think about what happened, both the thought of hurting him and the thought of revealing my gift."

"He seemed to be a spirit. I doubt whether you could've really hurt him," suggested Colin.

"They appear as an astral spirit and they can also materialize and are very much like us," said Bobby. "I saw two of them once at a funeral. That was another time I got mad and almost confronted them face to face."

"What happened?"

"This incident bothered me for months," said Bobby. "Like I said before, fairies like to mock humans. A mock funeral was taking place alongside the funeral for my great uncle Bob. Fairies were dressed in very colorful clothes and eating food from the banquet area prepared by the local church. Two fairy doubles materialized and approached my twin cousins; they started talking to them. My cousins were four years old at the time. Of course, I was the only person to know about the imposters. I felt blood rushing to my head as if I was going to pass out. The boys were in the hallway while their parents were paying their last respects.

I walked directly to my cousins with an angry look on my face. The fairies saw me and left the children making their way to the exit. I followed them, but as they left the building, they turned into a black mist, not realizing that I knew they were doppelgangers. The boys could not tell me what they had said to them."

"Could they be extraterrestrials from outer space?" asked Colin.

"I've thought about that too," said Bobby. "Perhaps fairies are aliens who discovered we have a soul and they want it. They are so advanced; they can live in our parallel world, travel back and forth and take anything they want."

"Aliens certainly would understand wormholes, parallel universes and time/space travel," suggested Colin. "Anything is possible. Have you ever had any good second sights?"

"I did have one encounter, but it was not a result of the gift."

"Tell me about it."

"I was fifteen. I took a walk in the woods behind my grandparents' home. It was a warm summer day so I went down to the creek to cool off. I sat on a rock and put my feet in the water. A beam of light broke through the trees shining on a rock on the opposite side of the creek, just a few feet away from me. There were sparkles and a fairy girl appeared before me sitting on the rock. She was dressed in yellow and gave me a sad smile.

I smiled back and asked her, "Could you be friends with a human?"

"Love conquers all," she said. "I can be your special friend and visit you any time you want. You enjoy the forest and the sunlight dancing on the stream as I do. We could explore nature together and appreciate the good things of the earth."

"Why do you want to be my friend," I asked.

"I have to be honest," she said sadly. "Your soul is what I want." Another beam of light broke through the trees next to her. Nothing else materialized; the girl dissipated into sparkles and was gone. That was my only conversation with a fairy. I never saw her again."

"Wow! Was she a babe? You could've had a girlfriend from out of this world. The second beam was probably her mother."

"Thanks for not giving me a hard time about all this fairy talk."

"I understand this is very serious and not easy for you," consoled Colin. "I want to find out everything I can about them. I want to read those dreams again, the rest of your journal, and see what I can find on the internet."

"One thing you'll learn on the internet is that I have broken the first rule about fairies," said Bobby.

"What's that?"

"The first rule is you never talk about them. You can read my journal, but you have to be very careful. Never leave it left open for any eyes to see."

"I'll be very careful. I look at this as scientific discovery. We'll get some answers."

"Thanks for listening and not being judgmental."

"Well," said Colin with a smile, "I always knew you were nuts, now I know why." They laughed and headed back to the beach house for the night.

CHAPTER 20

Letting Them In

Bobby could not relax that evening. After a tough week with final exams and sharing his secret with Colin, he was exhausted. Colin had one question after another. Finally, Bobby escorted his friend to the computer and told him to have fun with his research. Colin worked through the night exploring the legend of Minister Kirk, the Knights Templar, Dante's *Inferno*, and any information related to the history of fairies and their mythology in different cultures. He worked all night just as he had been doing for exams the past week. Sleeping on the beach the next day would not be a problem.

Fortunately, that evening, Petal Hailfrost, one of Khalen's guards assigned to monitor Bobby, was shirking her responsibilities; she was busy attempting to make connections at the boardwalk. Consulting with troubled girls and teasing young men were far more interesting than spending another evening with Bobby after a week of exams. She fully understood that the beginning of summer vacation was the best opportunity to connect with young people eager for excitement.

Having spent the entire night on the boardwalk, Petal rushed back to the beach house in the start of morning twilight. She was delighted with her assignment; with a little luck, she would gain some information about Bobby or Colin during a twilight dream. She had confidence in her skills to reach the subconscious mind to get information in the moments when a dream ends and the person awakens.

As Petal reached the beach house, she was thinking how Colin was more vulnerable than Bobby was; he was girl crazy and his scientific mind made him curious. To her delight, she found Colin still working on the computer. She diminished her size and carefully floated over his shoulder to see what he was doing. He was reading an article on how to meet a fairy. This amused and flattered her. The article explained how to set the mood, how to keep an open mind, and the importance of keeping the encounter private. Once Colin finished the article, he switched his research to read about a beautiful selkie. She was a fairy maiden from the sea who married a human hunter only to have a tragic ending.

Colin finished reading the tale and turned off the computer. The sunrise gave the room an orange glow and Colin looked out the front door to the ocean and smiled. He grabbed a beach towel, his music box, and a beer from the fridge and started out the door.

Feeling flirtatious, Petal blew an exotic feather that floated in front of Colin just as he went through the door. Nearly dropping his beer, Colin caught the feather. He had read that fairies love simple gifts like feathers and shells; the feather could help him with his experiment to set the mood and make contact. He thought it was wise to try an experiment since he was giving up his summer job. Petal knew what he was doing and was thrilled about the feather.

"Where are you going this early?" called Bobby coming from his bedroom.

Petal left the area quickly knowing Bobby had the gift of second sight.

"The only way I'll get any understanding about any of this is to examine things closely," replied Colin. "I don't know a wizard; I don't have a tether of hair and a funeral won't be possible. I am going to take this beer and a feather and try to meet one of those cuties at the ocean. Do you think I'll get lucky?"

"I think you'll finally get some sleep," said Bobby stepping outside. "What's this look on your face? I have seen it before. Oh, you have had an information overload. Enjoy the sunrise. I'm going back to bed."

From the beach, Petal could see the two of them talking. She danced with the ocean waves and did not take her eyes off Colin as he walked to a smooth sandy spot under the pier, a perfect place to set the mood.

He started with some soothing music; it blended well with the rhythm of the waves. The gentle breeze from the ocean did not allow him to place his feather in the middle of the beach towel. Petal caused a shell to wash on shore. Colin retrieved it and used the shell to secure the feather. After consuming the beer, he assumed a yoga position in front of the shell and feather and began to meditate; he attempted to clear his mind and focus on the sounds of the music and waves.

Closing his eyes, he heard a breathy voice say, "I am here for you." Opening his eyes, he caught a quick glimpse of Petal Hailfrost. She made eye contact; with a flicker of her pale blue eyes and a shake of her blonde hair, frosted at the tips like sparkles, she disappeared for a moment. Colin saw her legs as she dove into a wave breaking in the ocean.

He rubbed his eyes for it happened so quickly. She never surfaced. Sunlight on the waves flickered; another wave crashed close to shore; what just happened? He looked down and to his amazement, the feather, and shell was gone. In their place was a smooth white stone. Petal stood behind him smiling until Colin spoke, "We're coming to Fairy Knowe," he said aloud.

Petal was stunned. She immediately disappeared to return to the palace; Khalen needed to know this. Within moments, she passed through a portal and dashed to the garden underneath the ministers' tree. Khalen and Lilliana were enjoying two colorful chameleons walking through their flower garden when Petal rushed in with her news.

"Greetings to you, my king and queen; I have some troubling news for you. The boys I have been tracking, Bobby Kirk and Colin Campbell, are coming to Fairy Knowe."

"How do you know this, Petal?" asked Khalen.

"Colin told me they were coming," said Petal.

"Told you?" asked Lilliana. "You were supposed to track them. How is that possible?"

"He wanted to meet me and I gave him a bit of a tease," explained Petal. "It was very brief and he probably thinks it was the spirits he was drinking; but, he said they were coming here."

"How is it he wanted to see you?" asked Khalen.

"Not me, per se," said Petal, "he wanted to meet a fairy after a night of research."

"We may have found the minister's ancestor," said Lilliana. "We must be sure."

"Tell me about these young men," requested Khalen.

"They are college men on their summer break," explained Petal. "The taller one is smarter and crazy about girls, while the shorter one, Bobby Kirk, is serious and boring."

"He could be boring because he may know when you are around. I have very little information about this Kirk. Are the boys wealthy? How are they able to live at the beach?" asked Khalen. "Tell me something important about them."

"They are not wealthy," said Petal. "For their summers they work as lifeguards."

"Petal," said Khalen, "you must take Honey Driftsfur with you and set a trap to find out whether Bobby Kirk has the gift of second sight. I do not want you to do anything else but to set the trap and tell me how he responds. As lifeguards neither one of them would let a poor helpless soul drown. Do you understand?"

"I know exactly what to do," Petal answered.

High in the tree, the ministers heard the conversation. "His friend's name is Colin," stated Kirk Jr, surprised if not stunned. "Your eldest son, my brother Colin, would be happy to know this. They have found our ancestor."

"We must pray for them," said the father.

Bobby went to the beach around noon and found Colin sleeping under the boardwalk. He heard music playing and recognized the tunes. Colin was snoring with his right hand holding the stone from Petal. Under the corner of his beach towel was an empty can of beer. He gave Colin a tap on his shoulder to wake him and then spotted a swimmer at a distance off shore.

"Colin, wake up," said Bobby. "There's a swimmer far out to sea and about to have serious problems."

Colin woke up and jumped to his feet to see what was happening.

"I see him," said Colin, "but he looks fine. He is a little far out there. What do you see?"

"There's a double-man on him and it looks like foul play. "I've got to get there. The fairy is mocking and taunting him. He won't last much longer."

Bobby dove in the water and swam faster than he had ever done before. The doppelganger continued its harassment on the swimmer, even as Bobby reached him.

"I see you," shouted Bobby. "Leave this poor man alone," but the fairy continued. Bobby secured the victim; he had all the symptoms of having a stroke. With the skills of an astute lifeguard, Bobby swam to shore with the doppelganger still mocking the stroke victim. Paramedics pulled the man out of the water and onto a stretcher. Colin had called for help.

The fairy stayed close to the victim the whole time. Bobby lay exhausted on the shore and continued making eye contact with the doppelganger until the fairy gave him a big smile and disappeared. Bobby smacked the sand with both fists.

"What happened?" asked Colin.

"I just made a big mistake; the doppelganger knew clearly I could see him," said Bobby. "They know who I am. I've been baited into a trap."

"You saved the man's life, Bobby," said Colin. "No one else could have done that."

"I lost my temper," said Bobby. "Never before has one of them been so bold. They must have heard me tell my story and are now tracking me. I've always been so careful."

"I may have more bad news," said Colin. "This stone in my hand is from a fairy. I tried an experiment using information from the computer. I had an encounter; I saw a beautiful girl; her eyes were blue and she flirted with me. I followed the suggestion on the internet and had a feather and shell for a gift; she took them and left me this stone."

"You were up all night reading about that stuff and had a beer before you finally passed out," said Bobby. "That's not very scientific."

"I know it sounds crazy," said Colin showing him the stone, "but I know what I saw and this is evidence."

"We need to be very careful," said Bobby. "I don't like any of this. If you want to back out of the trip to Scotland, you still have time to cancel your flight."

"I'm sorry if I brought this on," said Colin.

"You didn't cause this to happen. My dreams have become intense; this would have happened without your experiment."

"You're going to need some help," said Colin. "I'm with you the whole way. Besides, that girl was beautiful, Bobby. I'm all in on this trip."

"Did you really think she'd fall for a feather and a shell? Have I not taught you anything about babes?"

"She seemed to like the presents," countered Colin.

"She left you cold as a stone," said Bobby and slapped his friend gently on the cheek. Colin put the stone in the pocket of his bathing suit and smiled.

"I promise to be more careful."

"I need to be more careful, too."

CHAPTER 21

A Gift Received in the Nick of Time

As soon as Bobby made eye contact with the doppelganger, Petal and Honey returned to Fairy Knowe. They went directly to Khalen's war room where he was analyzing data.

"Bobby Kirk has the gift of second sight just like the minister in our tree," said Petal.

"The young Kirk made eye contact with the double-man," added Honey. "He became very angry and began to swim to the victim before the victim needed help. He must be the ancestor of Robert E. Kirk, the one in your vision."

"His friend, Colin, who I told you about, had no idea what was happening," continued Petal. "I met him on the beach; we have a relationship. I can get more information for you. They are coming to Fairy Knowe."

"Petal, I can see you are fond of this Colin," commented Khalen. "Is there any indication Kirk carries or possesses an iron weapon?"

"There has never been an aura around him to indicate any presence of iron," said Petal.

"I have enough information to make my decision," said Khalen. "We must capture Bobby Kirk. He is a threat to our mission and a threat to our way of life."

"Colin mentioned Fairy Knowe, but of course, he meant Doon Hill," stated Honey. "They have no means to travel between the worlds. The young Kirk wants to come to Doon Hill with the hope of finding Fairy Knowe just like his ancestor."

"The minister carried an iron knife for protection," added Khalen. "Had he drawn the knife he would have broken my electromagnetic hold. With no iron weapon, this capture would be easy. A voluntary entrance into our world would fulfill my vision. Perhaps we can make their journey here much shorter. We simply must take advantage of a vulnerable moment."

"Colin seems very vulnerable," offered Lilliana. "Should he follow Petal through a gateway, Bobby would surely follow him."

"They have dates for Saturday night and flight arrangements for Monday," stated Petal. "Perhaps I could lure them into a portal after their dates, or during their flight. Both situations create vulnerability."

"Colin may follow you, but Bobby would be more wary," cautioned Khalen. "Honey, you must go with Petal and help her. Luring Colin into a portal may be possible, but Honey, you would need to push Bobby. I will be available should you need my help. Do not make the mistake of letting this young Kirk see either of you. Frightening him will make the task more difficult. A confrontation with Bobby Kirk is my destiny. When and how this occurs is to be determined, but there can be only one result. Bobby will join his ancestors in the pine."

"We will keep our distance until the right opportunity comes along," said Honey. "The area is crowded with fair folk seeking connections. It would be impossible for Bobby to know who we are even though Colin has made a connection with Petal."

"What will you do with Colin?" asked Petal.

"You will help with his brainwashing," said Khalen. "I have new information to manage their fears and temptations. He will learn to love our world. To remember his world would be intolerable and undesirable. Petal, he will be your responsibility until he adjusts. With his interest in science, he may be useful in a hospital or even with analyzing data."

At the beach house, Colin sat staring at his computer. "She's the most beautiful girl I've ever seen," he stated.

"Are you talking about the girls we're meeting tonight or the fairy who gave you a stone?" asked Bobby.

"There's no comparison; she's prettier than what I pictured from your journal," defended Colin. "She had blonde hair that sparkled and beautiful pale blue eyes. Did I tell you about her pouting lips? Are all fairies that beautiful?"

"You said these freshmen girls we're meeting tonight were the most beautiful girls you ever met."

"They are beautiful girls," said Colin. "This fairy girl is a babe."

"This fairy girl probably had something to do with that swimmer nearly drowning. In your research, did you not read about how they have lured men to their deaths?"

"I saw that, but I also read about some of them marrying humans and living wonderful lives together."

"You can have them," said Bobby. "I hope this trip will bring an end to my dreams and everything about them."

"In my research, I found the legend of your Gramps; it's exactly the same as your journal portrays. All your details are correct, even his appearance at the christening of his daughter. Much of the information from your dreams is historically correct. When we get to the tree, what will you do?"

"My only thoughts have been how my being there could relate to my dreams," said Bobby. "It seems impossible."

"Legend claims that if you run around the tree seven times you can see into their world. That's consistent with your dreams and the fairies making seven spins."

"I would feel silly doing that," said Bobby. "I guess I'm hoping for some kind of mental connection with him. Perhaps I'll know what to do when I get there."

"In the multiverse theory, similar to string theory, eleven dimensions started from the big bang. These dimensions are so close together like sheets of paper never touching. Any connection would be through a tunnel or wormhole. It appears to me that we need to build up centrifugal force with seven rotations to create a whirlpool. Since the two dimensions are connected, we could enter their world with a reversal of polarities. Seven rotations may be more important than speed. Fairy hunters at Doon Hill also make seven rotations around the tree, and they claim they can see through. I think we should experiment with the rotations when we get there."

"I don't know what you just said, but your experiments are going to get you in big trouble one day," cautioned Bobby. "But, I really appreciate your attention to all of this. I feel confident about finding some answers."

A knock at the door startled both of them. It was a postal delivery, express mail. Bobby signed a receipt for the special delivery.

"This must be the relic my grandparents promised me," said Bobby as he opened it. He found a note with some money wrapped around a small wooden box.

"This dough will come in handy for tonight," said Bobby while tucking the money into his pocket.

He read the note aloud: *This ring has been in our family since the time of Minister Robert E. Kirk. Legend claims that a knight gave this to our family for protection from the fairy folk. It didn't work for your great grandfather, but we hope you find it to be interesting as you explore our family tree, no pun or pine intended, Love Grammy and Pappy.*

"That's funny," said Colin. "Your grandparents have a good sense of humor.

"It's a ring on a chain," said Bobby. "It looks centuries old."

"Put in on," said Colin. "Wear it like a crucifix. Girls like guys with chains around their necks."

Bobby put the chain around his neck; the Holy Nail rested against his chest. Immediately he felt a familiar calming sensation, but made no connection with his dreams. It was like all the stress of the world was off his shoulders. A profound peace came over him.

He looked at his friend and said, "I want to go see the ocean. I can't describe how I feel; it's like my Gramps just put his hand on my shoulder, only more than that."

They walked to the ocean, to the location where they were earlier that day. Just before they reached the boardwalk, Petal Hailfrost and Honey Driftsfur re-entered this world through a gateway. They saw Bobby and Colin coming toward them and ducked out of sight.

"We are in luck," said Honey. "If we can get them here at the gateway, we may be able to make quick work of this."

"I will distract Colin from under the boardwalk," suggested Petal. "Once he follows me to the portal, you can give Bobby a push. Can you see how close they are to us?"

Honey peaked around the corner; she was repulsed at what she saw, "Bobby has an offensive green aura," she said. "This is not good. He must be carrying an iron weapon."

Petal peeked around the corner and saw the same greenish glow, "Oh my," she said, "he looks sickly. Perhaps it is a big knife or a gun. What should we do?"

"He has never carried anything like that before," said Honey. "We cannot do anything now. Perhaps he will leave it behind this evening when they go on their dates. We must be patient."

Honey quickly returned to Fairy Knowe and gave Khalen the news about the aura, obviously coming from an iron weapon. Within moments she returned to Petal; she was nauseous from simply watching Bobby. They took turns dealing with the offensive aura as they watched and listened for any news. Bobby and Colin stood on the shore looking across the ocean.

"I'm an ocean away and a world apart from my Gramps," said Bobby. "Since I put this chain on I feel like I'm closer than ever to him."

The two friends stood in silence for several minutes taking in the breeze and the rhythm of the waves before returning to the beach house. Petal and Honey followed them keeping their distance.

CHAPTER 22

JİLTED AND JOLTED

At dusk, a silvery white moon rose over the ocean. Bobby could see fairies dancing with excitement over the sparkling rays of light on the ocean waves. He could see their anticipation in making connections that evening with the multitude of young people on the boardwalk, along the beach and all over. Already, some young people were releasing pent up emotions, tasting freedom in a way they had never experienced. Only Bobby could see the fairies amongst them, studying their behavior and every word and looking for an opportunity to bond. He had observed this many times before.

Bobby and Colin headed toward their rendezvous point for their dates. It was a rooftop café overlooking the ocean across from the pier and new rollercoaster, the *Reverse Loop*. In no way did Bobby suspect that Khalen's guards, Petal Hailfrost and Honey Driftsfur, were tracking them. The two fairies kept their distance among the crowd. Petal changed the color of her hair and appearance in general, in the event that Colin had given Bobby a good description of her. Before reaching their destination, Bobby reminded Colin not to talk about fairies directly and not to refer to them. Their ability to blend in was perfect among those without the gift of second sight, and there were just too many fairies around.

They entered the boardwalk at the corner of the pier. An arcade was to their left with the rooftop café above it. They climbed the stairs; a waitress greeted them and gave them seats by the railing overlooking the boardwalk, pier, and ocean. The

175

moon was full; it looked much larger than usual. They had a clear view of everyone passing below, making it easy to call out to their dates when they arrived.

Honey and Petal loved the location. The arcade and rollercoaster were busy locations making it easy to keep an eye on Bobby and Colin without drawing any attention. From a distance, they could better deal with the unpleasantness of Bobby's green aura for he was still wearing the Holy Nail. Their only disadvantage was an inability to hear them.

"It is hard to believe that Bobby can see all of us," commented Honey.

"He sees what we see," agreed Petal. "This is so unusual. We cannot give him any idea we are following him."

"Perhaps we should send someone to tease them as a distraction for us?"

"That is an awful idea," said Petal. "If anyone is going to tease Colin, it will be me; besides, no one would flirt with Bobby."

"You are jealous, Petal. This is a very important mission and you have to stay professional."

"This has the potential of being a very frustrating evening," said Petal. "I do not like covering my hair. Colin, no doubt, described everything about me to Bobby."

"Be patient," said Honey. "Most dates, like the one they have planned, do not work out well. Once Colin is sad that his dream date is not his dream girl, you will be able to catch him on the rebound. Think about it. He will be crushed and will likely return to the spot where you met and think about you. Our portal is there. We make quick work of getting them through the tunnel and our work is done for today. You have to think positive."

"What if the date is wonderful and they really like each other? I will not be the one to say goodnight to him."

"If that happens, then tomorrow, we will meet them at their favorite spot under the boardwalk. They will be so happy that we will be able to coax them into the gateway there."

"How will we do that?"

"I have my tricks just like you do," said Honey.

"Let us take turns watching them," said Petal. "Do you see the young girl out there on the sand looking at the moon? I know that look; she has issues. This will not take very long. I have to get to her before someone else does. See you later."

Time seemed to stop for Honey, but she understood Petal's desire to make a connection. Watching the boys without making eye contact and keeping an eye on Petal was more difficult than she expected. Everyone on the boardwalk was having fun but her. She wondered what Bobby and Colin were talking about and whether Petal was going to return in time to help her. Becoming more and more concerned as to how all this would work; she realized that Bobby had a weapon and the ability to see her. She would be the one in great danger should something go wrong. Different scenarios and options ran through her mind.

Colin was excited about meeting his date, but foremost in his mind and in the palm of his hand was Petal's stone. His research had produced a most amazing experience.

"Are we free to talk at this table," asked Colin.

"This is a good location to talk. I can see a lot of activity, but we are alone. I do not see a beautiful blonde with pale blue eyes and pouting lips. I'll let you know if a fairy comes in our direction."

"I wonder if I'll ever see her again," said Colin. "Anyway, I'm convinced the key to passing through a wormhole is controlling the electromagnetic fields at the time of connection. Electromagnetic grids run around the earth like a road map. I've heard that extraterrestrials use this energy; perhaps they are the same. Places like Stonehenge, the pyramids and Doon Hill in Scotland are at the crossroads of electromagnetic grids. This beach area is also a prime location for electromagnetic energy."

"Let me see if I understand you," said Bobby. "Are you saying our parallel worlds are closer to each other at different locations because of the flow of energy?"

"That's what I'm saying," said Colin. "In places like the Bermuda Triangle, airplanes and boats may get caught in some centrifugal motion either in the air or water and end up in the parallel world."

"That's wild," said Bobby.

"What else is wild is the eleven dimensions of the string theory are measurable and began at the moment of the big bang, the creation of our universe. To travel between parallel worlds I think you need to find a point where electromagnetic energy is high, create some kind of whirlpool effect with seven rotations, and then enter a portal or gateway by reversing kinetic energy."

"I get it," said Bobby. "Find a high-energy spot, spin like a top, put it in reverse, and walk in like we own the place."

"Exactly," said Colin, "I couldn't have said it better. From reading about those gateways or tunnels into Hell, I think that passing into each world must be different. Electromagnetic waves impact our brains in many ways. Passing through a wormhole could be very strange. While the distance is only a few millimeters, a journey could seem long. Your journeys through the gateways seemed like they took a fair amount of time. I can only imagine how you feel when these dreams occur."

"I just want them to stop. While I recognize they are only dreams, they are unnerving. It sounds like you have a good idea as to what is going on. My Gramps was a brave pioneer to enter their world."

"I'm convinced he stumbled on a method that's not very complicated. He's given you clues in your dreams."

"It's just that the dreams are driving me nuts."

"We'll get some answers and you'll be fine. We know a gateway exists at Doon Hill near the Fairy Tree. Perhaps we'll meet someone who has looked into the parallel world."

"Hold that thought," said Bobby. "I see our dates; they're with guys."

"Oh, man, we've been replaced," said Colin. "Look at the beasts they're with!"

"The guy with your date must be six feet six and three hundred pounds."

"I know who he is. He is an ultimate fighter from the octagon. The fellow he is with looks like a clone. Go say something to them."

"Are you kidding?" said Bobby. "Those guys could kill us. I never really liked the blonde anyway."

"Oh well, perhaps we'll meet a couple of lasses in Scotland."

"Let's forget about our dates and give the *Reverse Loop* a spin," suggested Colin.

The girls made eye contact with Bobby and Colin knowing they would be there. As if they planned it, they each gave their heavyweight date a kiss, and walked into the arcade arm in arm.

Honey Driftsfur witnessed the exchange. For a moment, she felt bad for the boys, but quickly realized, this was their opportunity.

Bobby and Colin were obviously very disappointed; their self-esteem had taken a hard hit. They left the balcony café with their heads down and got in line for a ride on the Reverse Loop.

Honey surveyed the rollercoaster hoping to find a portal. The coaster carried its riders to a high point and then reversed directions. At the highest point Honey spotted a rare multiport, a special type of wormhole headed toward indefinite locations. She could not believe her luck in finding this rare portal, the closest point to connecting their worlds. Even though they could end up anywhere, it would be very easy to pass through.

The opportunity to make quick work of their assignment was there. She and Petal only needed to meet the boys at the pinnacle of the ride and take them through the gateway to Fairy Knowe. Although Bobby had a green aura from some kind of iron weapon, he would be strapped into the coaster and unable to break the electromagnetic charge to complete the journey.

Honey looked to Petal and waved her arms, but to no avail. Petal was in a deeply private conversation with a young girl, Sophie, the kind of conversation every faerie desired and no faerie would dare interrupt. Honey was desperate; she needed Petal's help.

CHAPTER 23

PETAL'S DISTRACTIONS

The moonlit ocean and the soft boom of whitecaps breaking at sea made the moment perfect for Petal to connect with Sophie, an innocent, unsuspecting soul confused about her future and the prospect of having a boyfriend for the summer. Petal sent a message on the warm summer breeze for Sophie to speak aloud her thoughts and feelings.

"My clothes, my hair, my nails, my personality, I hate everything about me," mumbled Sophie to the moon.

"I hear you," said Petal in a gentle voice carried by the warm ocean breeze. "I am here for you and have your spirit at heart. You need me. Beauty, glamour, love, and passion are complicated. Promise me you will never speak to anyone about me, and I will help you get what you desire. You can trust me and depend on me."

"Who are you? What are you?" questioned Sophie in a whisper.

"You have heard of me. Many of the fairy tales you have heard have some truth behind them."

"I don't believe in fairies."

"Call me what you like. I will just be your secret friend. I must have your promise never to speak of me before I can reveal myself to you. You have some very strong feelings you need to talk about."

"I have no style and I'm not pretty enough for him," replied Sophie to the gentle soothing voice.

"Promise me you will never speak to anyone about me," said Petal, "I will help you get what you desire."

"I can't see you," said Sophie responding to the voice. "Why should I trust you?"

"I speak only of things like beauty, glamour, love, and passion," said Petal. "Everyone desires these things; I would love to be your friend, and talk about these gifts of love. Do you love to talk about these things?"

"I know nothing about these things."

"We can talk openly about these things looking over the expanse of the ocean with the beautiful moon and lovely breeze; but, only if you promise to never speak to anyone about me. I bring great promise to you with your promise to me."

"I promise," said Sophie.

Petal made her grand appearance; she was a vision of style and grace. Reaching out her hands to Sophie, she touched her, "We will be friends for life," said Petal confidently. "Tell me what you desire. Beauty is life and love conquers all things."

Honey Driftsfur arrived on the beach at just that moment; she saw the look in Sophie's eyes and in no way could she interrupt the encounter. A delicate situation was before her. Fairies never interrupt a connection; building trust is so important, yet they were under orders from King Khalen to apprehend Bobby Kirk. Without hesitation, Honey flew to the multiport at the pinnacle of the *Reverse Loop* and returned to Fairy Knowe. Khalen was sitting in the circle garden anxiously awaiting any news.

"King Khalen," exclaimed Honey, "we have a unique situation. The blind dates jilted Bobby and Colin. To deal with their sadness, they are in line for a roller coaster ride. Here we have our good fortune; the ride reaches a pinnacle connecting with a multiport, an easy location to capture them. Although Bobby has the green aura, and therefore is carrying a weapon, he would be strapped into the ride and unable to use it. I could get Bobby through the tunnel with Petal taking Colin."

Khalen said nothing.

"Here is the problem," continued Honey. "Petal has made a perfect connection with a young girl. Her name is Sophie; I cannot break the trust she is creating. That could be disastrous. I need Petal's help to get both boys into the multiport. I am not afraid of Bobby and his weapon. The straps will keep him from using it. What should I do?"

"I am pleased you have come to me for advice, Honey," said Khalen. "This is a very tricky situation. I will go with you to help with the abduction. Petal needs to take care of Colin, while I am with you; Bobby Kirk may somehow use his weapon. I have an idea; it could help Petal maintain her trusting bond with Sophie and everything will be fine. We are so fortunate to have located a multiport in the area. You have done well."

Khalen paused for a moment and then directed his attention to the ministers high up in the tree, "Your incarcerations will not last much longer," he shouted. "Another Kirk is on his way to help me achieve my goals."

In an instant, Khalen and Honey Driftsfur circled the massive pine tree, entered a wormhole, and travelled to the multiport. They watched as Bobby and Colin got into a cart on the *Reverse Loop*. Petal was still engaged in her conversation with Sophie.

"I realize you may not think you are beautiful," said Petal to Sophie. "I know what is best for you."

Just then, an unmistakable shadow appeared on the beach. Petal recognized the figure of King Khalen with one arm raised; she immediately remembered her mission.

"Sophie, I want you to dye your hair green and purple; get a matching tattoo that reads *'Friends forever but never tell'*. I will meet you this same time tomorrow night and we will talk more. I suddenly feel ill and must think more about your issues. We will talk again tomorrow."

Sophie gave a big smile; Petal flickered away and headed directly to King Khalen.

"There is no time to discuss this," said Khalen. "We must go to Honey now."

Within a few moments, Khalen and Petal were at the pier. "The boys have boarded the ride," said Honey. "They will travel in the coaster backward in a loop and shoot straight up to the sky on a rail. Petal, when they reach the pinnacle, you will appear before Colin to his right and I will appear before Bobby to his left to have them looking in opposite directions."

"I will be with Honey," added Khalen. "We will escort the young Kirk through the multiport and return to Fairy Knowe. Take Colin through the portal to wherever it goes and then to a tropical location. Reassure him that everything will be fine, and that his dreams are coming true. We cannot take chances for him to remain behind. He will be useful to me."

While they were talking, the rollercoaster attendant strapped Bobby and Colin into a car on the *Reverse Loop*.

Colin said to the attendant, "Give us the maximum number of loops possible. We've just been jilted; a good jolt may take us to another world."

"I have a maximum jolt; it's been tested but never used in public," said the attendant. "This baby can push four g's. I bet the girls were blondes; weren't they?"

"They were cute blondes," admitted Bobby.

"Is four g's all you got?" asked Colin.

"I can detach your car from the others and give it the maximum of seven loops," said the attendant. "Can you handle that?"

"Seven loops will take us to another world," said Colin. "Give us everything you got."

The attendant laughed and detached the car. He reset the power and started the ride; it began in a backward motion.

"You'll go backward for seven loops," shouted the attendant, "and then go straight to the top where you'll get a good view of the moon. Your stomach will leave this earth, but your body will return to me after going forward for seven more loops. Do you have any questions?"

"No questions," shouted Bobby.

"See you on the other side," said Colin.

The attendant set the car in motion; he blew a horn and set off a laser show to attract the crowd on the pier and boardwalk. The ride started slowly and picked up speed gradually.

"I've been studying electromagnetic energy all morning," said Colin. "My guess is we could travel to the parallel world if we could create a circular motion like a whirlpool effect in an electromagnetic grid. A reversal of kinetic energy may just send us through a portal. Let's try an experiment."

"You just want to see Petal Hailfrost," joked Bobby.

"Work with me on this one," said Colin. "When we get to the high point of this ride after the loops, let's both move our shoulders and head to the left at the same time to change our direction."

"What will we do if your experiment works? How will we get back?"

"It won't work, but perhaps we may see something unusual," said Colin. "I believe your ancestral grandfather looked into their world."

"What if you see Petal again?" asked Bobby. "Would that make you feel less jilted?"

"I'm going to Scotland with you," said Colin. "The least you could do is to try my experiment."

"I'll do it," said Bobby.

"When we get to the high point, I'll shout 'Reverse'," explained Colin. "With a quick snap, we'll turn our heads and shoulders to the left. This will start the reversal motion."

"I heard you the first time," said Bobby.

As the coaster spun faster and faster, the attendant continued to use his laser and horn to get the crowd's attention. The crowd started counting the number of loops. The manager of the *Reverse Loop* heard all the noise and became alarmed; he had not authorized his attendant to put the coaster at full throttle, and rushed to see what was happening.

"What are you doing?" asked the manager. "This is a dangerous stunt. We could be sued."

"Don't worry," said the attendant. "I know what I'm doing."

"This could be your last day on the job," said the manager.

The crowd continued their counting to the sixth and then seventh loop. Bobby and Colin left the loop at full speed shooting straight upward to the sky. Khalen, Honey Driftsfur and Petal Hailfrost darted from the boardwalk to meet them at the pinnacle. Colin shouted, "Reverse!"

They both looked at a stunned Petal Hailfrost and entered a dark corridor.

The single car coaster made its way back through the loops with the crowd counting each loop. When the car came to a stop, the manager's troubled look changed to a smile. He patted the attendant on the back; the car was empty.

"What a great advertisement stunt with no one on board," said the manager. "Look at that line to come in here. Instead of firing you, I'll give you a small raise. Next time tell me when you are going to pull a stunt like this. You're a genius."

"Thanks boss, I'm sorry I made you worry."

"I thought there were two fellas strapped in that car," said the next person in line. "Where did they go?"

"To the moon," said the manager, "or beyond."

"Or perhaps they went into the twilight zone," offered the next rider. Everyone laughed and the manager kept patting his employee on the back.

Petal, Honey, and King Khalen were stunned to see the boys disappear before their eyes. They looked at each other in total disbelief, knowing they could be anywhere in their world.

"I was in position to take him to a tropical island and then I looked into his puppy eyes," said Petal. "They disappeared before I could do anything."

"They could be anywhere," stated Khalen. "The options are infinite. I must return home immediately and start a search."

The boys were now missing persons; only the attendant was aware of this. He was not about to say anything for fear of the possibility of losing a raise in pay, let alone his job.

Family expected the boys to be off to Europe; it could be a couple of weeks before they would call home. It would be a while before anyone would be concerned about them; they were young men wanting their space.

Never in any of Bobby's wildest dreams did he imagine this happening. Bobby and Colin knew only that they had passed through a portal. They both recognized Petal Hailfrost, Colin from the beach and Bobby from his dreams. Her frosted hair was unique even with fairies. Through Colin's experiment, they had discovered a connection between our parallel worlds. The worlds are now connected like never before.

"Imagination is more important than knowledge."
EINSTEIN

Acknowledgements

Marie Kneuker *my loving wife*

Melli Marie - *Daughter/critic*

James Kneuker - *Son/critic*

Patricia Jepsen - *Artwork*

Candice M. Carta-Myers - *Graphic Designer and Project Manager*

Nancy Dickson - *Copyeditor*

Dr. John Manhold - *Mentor*

About the Author

Clark Kneuker graduated with honors from Northeastern University, completing majors in Psychology and English. Prior to that, he served in the U.S. Air Force and earned a small-arms expert marksmanship ribbon. He served in a tour of duty in Vietnam. He met his wife, Marie, while stationed in Spain. They have two talented children Melli and Jim.

His career as a social worker with Child Protective Services and a Probation Officer was with the State of Delaware. For a career change, he then attended Delaware Technical Community College earning a degree in Business Administration with honors. This led to a second career in banking with MBNA.

Clark stumbled across the idea for these stories during an attempt to write an English play for his daughter in London.

Melli,
Thank you for all your input to helping me in this project. Your mother and me consider you and Jim as our greatest achievements. Love Dad

189

About the Artist

Patricia Jepsen, from Rising Sun, Maryland, trained at the University of Delaware, University of North Florida

Patricia had an early love of Art. However, she began her professional life as a model in New York, Chicago, Philadelphia.

She later studied Psychology and went on to a full time career working with University students. She retired in 2002 and returned to her first passion.

Patricia's painting gained public attention when picked up by the CBS Sunday Morning Show as a promo for the Meryl Streep film "Florence".

Her vibrant work is gaining popularity in the States and Abroad. As she has just returned from a solo Art Exhibition in London, England at the prestigious Park Theatre, where she was commissioned to paint a portrait of the world renowned actor Ian McKellan. The Star of Lord of the Rings. Her art work is usually notable for the Eyes which are a key feature in her work. This flows from her aim to reflect a person's soul. This is why we loved having her as the illustrator of the "Parallel Worlds".

References

Morey, T., 2008. *The Fairy Bible*, 1st ed. 387 Park Avenue South New York, NY 10016. Sterling Publishing Inc.

Kirk R., 2008. *The Secret Commonwealth of Elves, Fauns and Fairies* Dover Ed. Mineola, New York. Dover Publications.

Kirk's book was originally published in 1815 at the behest of Sir Walter Scott.

Printed in Great Britain
by Amazon